"You must marry me."

Prescott's voice was as passionate as his embrace, but Eleanor's reaction surprised even him.

"Odious, odious man!" she half sobbed, half laughed. "How dare you! Do you think I am no better than a trollop? Love me? You cannot love anyone. You are too vain, selfish, self-serving."

Prescott caught her fists in his hands and kissed them.

"I beg you let go of me, sir," Eleanor said coldly. "I find this entire spectacle revolting."

"Revolting!" Prescott's temper flared. He had humbled himself in front of her and this is the way she treated him. "Very well," he answered. "You'll hear not another word from me."

He flung down her wrists and turned away, then just as abruptly he turned back to her and snatched her up, crushing his lips down on hers.

Taken by surprise, Eleanor had hardly time to think let alone fight him off, and one part of her, the treacherous side, did not want to fight him off. His kiss was all that she remembered it was, intoxicating, breathtaking, a promise of what could be. She met his passion with hers, never for a moment considering the consequences.

As abruptly as he had taken her, Prescott pushed her away.

"I trust you did not find that *too* revolting, my dear," he said, barely able to contain his wrath.

As Eleanor watched him stride away, her only answer was a sob.

Books by Clarice Peters

HARLEQUIN REGENCY ROMANCE

PRESCOTT'S LADY
CLARICE PETERS

Harlequin Books

TORONTO • NEW YORK • LONDON
AMSTERDAM • PARIS • SYDNEY • HAMBURG
STOCKHOLM • ATHENS • TOKYO • MILAN

for Adrian, again

Published April 1990

ISBN 0-373-31123-0

CHAPTER ONE

LADY CONSTANCE WHITING lifted a cup of Bohea tea to her lips and discreetly scanned the latest on-dits occupying the back pages of the *Morning Post*, a subterfuge necessitated by the presence in the breakfast parlour of her sister-in-law, Lady Vyne.

Had she known Lavinia would descend upon her just as she was about to partake of her breakfast, Lady Con would have ordered a tray in her room. Knowing her sister-in-law only too well, she had instead fortified herself with another sip of Mr. George Berry's excellent blend of tea and prepared for a long siege. When the mood was upon her, Lavinia could outtalk even Lady Jersey. Perhaps, Lady Con thought as she smoothed the napkin on the lap of her lavender day dress, a touch of the grippe might induce Lavinia to leave. Fortunately, before she was obliged to resort to such desperate measures, a tall, sandy-haired gentleman strolled into the room.

"Andrew, my dear." Lady Con waved her son in with an excess of enthusiasm. "Have you arrived for our outing in the Park? Wicked one, you come far too early, but I shall be ready in a trice. You don't mind, Lavinia, do you?"

Mr. Andrew Whiting met his mother's imploring look with a twinkle in his own eyes as he bent to peck her on a powdered cheek.

"Mama, you are a minx."

Lady Constance heaved a sigh of relief. Thank heavens Andrew was no slow top, but then she had been blessed with the finest son and daughter imaginable. Andrew, the elder, resembled her the most, with the same wheat-coloured hair, brilliant blue eyes and even temperament. Highly intelligent, Andrew was the author of several pamphlets on scientific matters.

Eleanor, his sister, was accomplished too. Her own small book of poems had enjoyed an enthusiastic response among the literati of London. What was more important in a female, she was also acknowledged to be a diamond of the first water.

"But, Constance—" Lady Vyne's protest cut into these maternal musings "—you can't go for your ride just yet. I haven't had a chance to talk to you."

Lady Constance choked as she put down her Sèvres teacup, unwilling to accept this charge with equanimity. "You've been talking to me for well over an hour," she declared.

Colouring slightly, Lady Vyne plucked at the fraise about her neck with agitated fingers.

"Yes, I know, but I didn't tell you the most important news," she paused, perceiving two pairs of eyes rivetted on her face and prepared to shed the last vestige of pretense about her morning visit. "I'm giving a ball for Maria."

"Who?" Andrew asked, helping himself to a scone. His mother's warning glance came too late. Lavinia prided herself on being the family historian and inhaled a majestic breath, ready to delineate in exhaustive detail the relationship between Maria Whiting and their branch of the family.

"A cousin," Lady Constance said, cutting short this ramble through her husband's family tree. "Lavinia has charge of her for the season, and I wish you success in finding her a suitable match."

"Oh, do you really mean that?" Lavinia asked, seizing upon these innocent words with a fervour that surprised mother and son. "Because I have invited all the eligibles. Here is a list." She laid a cream-coloured sheet in front of her sister-in-law. "I do want Maria to make a brilliant match."

The pair of blue eyes idly scanning the paper came to a stricken halt.

"Good heavens, Lavinia. You can't be serious!" Lady Constance exclaimed. "You can't mean to invite Prescott to your ball for Maria."

"If I am to marry her off I must invite all the eligible partis here in London," Lavinia protested. "And Prescott is of impeccable lineage as well as handsome and as wealthy as Golden Ball."

Lady Constance snorted, needing no reminder about Prescott's standing in the ton since she had become well acquainted with that very background and fortune three years ago when he had nearly married Eleanor.

"It won't do, Aunt Lavinia," Andrew said now, plucking up the invitation list and scrutinizing it through his quizzing glass as though it were a specimen under his microscope.

"And why not?" Lady Vyne asked, not about to give up without a fight.

"The prattleboxes would never stop. Everyone knows he and Eleanor have been at cross points ever since she broke off their engagement three years ago."

Lady Constance rose like an incubus from her chair. "That man! I vow, I have forbidden anyone to speak his name in my presence. When I think of the way he treated Eleanor."

"Heavens, if I remember correctly she gave as good as she got," Lavinia said, having the word with no bark on it. "I'm not saying he wasn't a rake, for he was, but no lady of breeding would send his engagement ring back to him wrapped in a bit of muslin!"

Lady Constance winced. She'd hoped that three years' time would have dulled everyone's memory of her daughter's behaviour—behaviour she herself had never fully understood. Against her will, she found her thoughts returning to Prescott's courtship of her daughter in the spring of 1813.

Lord Prescott was one of Society's handsomest and wealthiest gentlemen, used to reckless play both with his horses and at the green baize tables. Miss Eleanor Whiting was a beautiful, lively young lady determined not to add her heart to the trail of broken ones that littered Prescott's wake. Inevitably their paths crossed. The results had stood the ton on its ear.

Eleanor laughed off all his attempts to woo her, stoutly declaring to her friends and family that Lord Prescott was resting himself before he took the arduous task of selecting a new *chère amie*, a statement that had shocked many but had highly amused Prescott.

But if rake Prescott was, he seemed bent on reformation during his courtship of Eleanor, even to the extent of appearing to waltz with her at Almack's. At last he had won her reluctant affection. Lady Constance herself was not immune to his charms, and he even fulfilled Lord Whiting's stringent requirements in a son-in-law.

The rake had reformed. Prescott bestowed his mother's gold-and-diamond ring upon Eleanor as a betrothal gift. Then, like a shot, the match was over. Eleanor returned home to Mount Street one day after an outing at Hampton Court looking like a regular bear jaw, and the very next morning she dispatched the ring to Prescott, wrapped, as Lavinia had so accurately recalled, in a bit of muslin.

Had the ring been sent to Prescott's residence and opened in private perhaps no scandal would have ensued. But the footman had met Prescott near St. James' Street and his lordship had opened the note and the ring in White's. The tale swept London, and he had become the butt of the Bond Street beaux. The ensuing bumblebroth had divided much of polite Society, some taking Prescott's side and others Eleanor's.

The three years had been difficult ones for hostesses forced to make the ticklish decision whether to invite Prescott or Eleanor to their various routs and soirées. Luckily Prescott had made a habit of going to his country estate for most of the Seasons past.

"If you have invited that man to your ball none of us shall be in attendance," Lady Constance said now, striding purposefully across her prized Wilton.

"But Constance, you must," Lavinia entreated, following after her like a wren trailing an eagle. "Only think what the scandalmongers will say if you are not present."

"Donald may attend in my absence, if he wishes it," Lady Constance said magnanimously, knowing full well her husband's dislike of balls, particularly his sister's. "And however much people will gossip if we absent ourselves, they will surely talk even more if we appear."

"Andrew, you and Julia will come, won't you?" Lavinia shifted her tactics to her nephew. "You have reached your majority and no longer live with your father, so you needn't quake if Donald gets on his high ropes," Lady Vyne pointed out.

"It's not Father's temper I'm afraid of. It's Eleanor's," Andrew said frankly. "She'll be mad as a bee, that much I do know."

"Shall I, Andy?" A voice laughed and the three occupants of the breakfast parlour turned to find the subject of their intent conversation standing in the arched doorway.

Dressed in a sable pelisse with a matching fur hat that she now pulled off, loosening a head of copper-coloured curls, Miss Eleanor Whiting made a fetching sight. Tall but not of such a height as to cause her shoulders to stoop, Miss Whiting was blessed with a creamy complexion unmarred by either spots or freckles. She dropped a kiss on her aunt's cheek and bade her brother to close his mouth.

"Lest one think you were catching flies."

"Oh, Eleanor, you are the very one we have been speaking of...I mean," Lavinia fluttered to a confused halt. "Oh dear, I had no idea. I wish I could retrieve the invitation. But I dispatched it earlier while I still had the courage. The deed is done.... How awkward."

Eleanor's hazel eyes passed from her aunt to her mother and finally focused on her brother. "Andrew, what is going on, pray?"

"Aunt Lavinia is giving a ball. She's invited Prescott," he said succinctly. This bare-bones recital of the facts which had taken Lady Vyne a full hour to divulge did not appear to shock Eleanor.

"I see," she said, dropping gracefully into a chair.

"Then you're not overset?" her aunt asked, peering anxiously into the lovely face in front of her.

A trace of a smile touched Eleanor's lips. "Heavens no, Aunt Lavinia. Invite whomever you like." Only the faint tremor in her fingers as she poured herself a cup of tea gave away her true feelings.

"There, I told you, Constance!" Lavinia crowed. "Eleanor is not such a poor creature as to begrudge Maria her chance with Prescott even though she herself failed to land him."

"It was Prescott who failed to win Eleanor." Lady Constance's voice lifted a mere fraction of an octave.

"That's what I said," Lavinia made haste to explain. "And I do hope that you all will come to the ball.

"Why, Aunt Lavinia, I wouldn't miss it for the world!"

Lady Vyne swept her into a scented embrace, pronounced her a veritable paragon and departed on a whirlwind of errands to be run.

"Eleanor, if you dislike the ball we needn't attend, any of us. I know how much you dislike Prescott," her mother said, trying to read that unfathomable look in her daughter's eyes.

"Don't be silly, Mama," Eleanor said with a laugh. "I don't dislike him. I'm utterly indifferent to him."

Neither her mother nor her brother quarrelled openly with her words, but both knew that she was shamming it. Prescott's effect on females of whatever age could never have evoked indifference. Even Lady Constance at the age of forty-three was obliged to recall how her pulse had raced ever so slightly when he had kissed her hand. And he had certainly kissed more than her daughter's hand.

Eleanor was every inch her mother's daughter, and no gentleman she had ever met had stirred so many emotions as did Prescott in his brief courtship of her. He was the most maddening, autocratic, witty, and handsome gentlemen she had ever known. Even now, and it had been three years, she could still summon up his face, the laughing brown eyes and the way his lips curved when he was genuinely amused. Less fondly she also recalled the autocratic glint in his eyes and the way they flashed when he was displeased. Yet there was a softer, warmer look when he held her close when they danced. And as for his kisses...

"Oh do stop thinking like a schoolroom miss," Eleanor admonished herself later as she lay on the great four-poster in her bedchamber.

She was a grown woman of twenty-three now. For that matter, she was not the only female to have sampled his kisses. No doubt his mistress of long standing, Aimée Martine, could speak on that particular topic at length.

THE DARK-HAIRED GENTLEMAN dressed in an exquisitely cut coat of sea-blue superfine with matching trousers descended the Adam staircase, halting only at the sight of his estimable secretary holding an invitation on a silver tray.

Mock horror crossed his craggy countenance as he picked up his York tan gloves from the buhl table at the bottom of the stairs. The day was brisk, and he had waiting a pair of Welshbreds long on speed and short on exercise.

"Not another theatrical or masque, Lynch," he said.

"No, my lord," answered Mr. Lynch. "It's a come-out party."

Lord Prescott lifted a shaggy brow. Either Arthur had gone daft or he had been overworked by the bills for Quarter Day. The day he'd be interested in any chit's come-out party would be a day he'd eat his new high-crowned beaver felt from Locke.

"My dear Lynch, why haven't you told me how overworked you've been? A quiet sojourn in the country is just what you need. I've just come from the country myself and deem it excellent for restoring one's sense of peace, if one doesn't die of boredom first. Or perhaps you would enjoy the waters at Bath."

"Good Jupiter, no, sir."

A smile crossed Prescott's face, lightening features which, while classically shaped with an aquiline nose, square jaw, and high brow, could appear stern in repose.

"I don't blame you, Lynch. I sampled the waters once myself. But if you're not sick what excuse do you have for telling me about some schoolroom miss's come-out?"

"Perhaps you ought to look at the invitation yourself, my lord," his secretary said in strangled accents.

With an indulgent smile, Prescott picked up the invitation and scanned the brief lines. His smile faded as the names Lord and Lady Vyne registered with him. "There must be an error. Vyne would never invite me."

"Oh no, my lord," Lynch said quickly. "I checked the invitation twice and went over to Green Street myself to enquire, civilly, I assure you, if there were any error."

And well he might, Prescott thought, slapping one York tan glove against another. Lady Vyne was Miss Whiting's aunt. Miss Eleanor Whiting, the female who had held him up to public scorn three years ago.

It seemed like yesterday. No lady he had ever met could equal Eleanor at making him laugh. Her smile was like a kiss of sunshine. He had thought he had discovered the perfect mate, one he could cherish and love. But that had come to naught. His jaw tightened as he remembered uncovering his ring nestled among the muslin.

How the bucks had roared. The perfect insult. She had played him for a fool, never intending to marry him, amusing herself at his expense, and when he had finally taken the step of declaring himself she had accepted, knowing full well that she would deliver the ultimate facer.

In three years he had not spoken her name to anyone, and no one dared to mention her to him. But now and then he saw mention of her in the columns of the *Morning Post*. She was still unwed, though the quizzes predicted Harry Addison was bursting to pop the question.

"What do you make of my receiving such an invitation, Lynch?" Prescott asked.

"It seems to me that this might be construed as a peace offering."

Prescott frowned. "Indeed. You detect Miss Whiting's hand behind this matter?"

"Sometimes one hesitates to apologize directly, so sets about doing so indirectly."

Direct or indirect, an apology was not Miss Whiting's style. She was out to amuse herself again, he'd go bail. His lips tightened. But three years had passed, and he was a far better opponent than before. It would be amusing to cross swords with her again, knowing that his heart was immune.

"Shall I send your regrets, my lord?" Lynch asked.

"Certainly not," Prescott replied, placing his high-crowned beaver felt carefully on his head. "I am never one to turn my nose up at a peace offering. I will attend with the greatest pleasure." And he set off to exercise his horses and visit his aunt.

"WELL, PETER, I see the quizzes are right," Mrs. Edgewater, a spry sixty-year old said as she greeted him in her blue drawing room.

"About what, Aunt Judith?" he asked, taking the seat next to her on the satinwood sofa. "That you are growing more beautiful every day?"

"Don't talk fustian nonsense," she said, her voice softening slightly as she gazed fondly at him. Dark-haired, tall, with the unmistakable air of Quality, he had occupied a special spot in her heart from the time he was in short coats. Corinthian though he was, he still found time to visit her monthly.

"You returned to London yesterday and have only come calling on me now."

"You wouldn't have liked to see me yesterday," he protested mildly. "I was in all my dirt."

"Which it took the better part of a day to wash off?" she asked ironically.

"Not if William, my valet, has a brush to wield. I vow, he left my back with scarcely any skin at all." Prescott stretched out his long legs and accepted a glass of sherry from the tray of restoratives the butler held out. "I know I have been remiss, Aunt Judith, but I did want to mull over what I found at Oakmore before I saw you. Yesterday I was too tired . . ."

"But after an evening at the green baize tables of White's, you are much refreshed?" she asked mildly.

Prescott nearly chucked his sherry down his shirt-front. "Aunt Judith, you are a griffin. And it wasn't White's or Watier's, but a card party at Edward Cassidy's."

"Edward," Mrs. Edgewater sniffed audibly. "Why do you associate with him? He's a loose screw and a rake."

"So am I, so I've been told."

His aunt stamped her ivory-handled cane. "You are no such thing. Who dared to utter such slander?"

"Eleanor Whiting, for one. My crimes are considerable if you believe her."

Mrs. Edgewater's face softened. "Oh, Peter, does her refusal still smart?"

"Heavens no," Prescott acted quickly to allay the pity in his aunt's eyes. "We wouldn't have suited. Fortunately we discovered that in time. Our marriage would have been a fatal miscue. And how did we wind up on such a tangent? I came here to report on your estate which I'm sorry to say, Aunt, is in a very bad way."

The next half hour passed with his answering her very astute questions concerning the extent of the necessary repairs and the cost of the same.

"You could bring it up to snuff but it will cost the earth. I know your pockets are deep."

"But not that deep," she said drily. "Well then, since I can't repair it without reducing myself to penury, a state I am loath to embrace at my advanced age, I shall sell it."

Although this was the very alternative that Prescott was about to suggest he was surprised that she could so easily choose it.

"I have had considerable time to mull it over," she told him wryly. "Since Frederick's death." She gazed over at the portrait of her husband by Sir Thomas Lawrence which dominated the room. "I am too old for the place. I thought that I might give it to you."

Prescott blinked in astonishment.

"As a wedding present," she explained. "That was back when you were dangling after Eleanor Whiting."

"Oh. I had no notion."

She pressed his hand with hers. "And since you haven't seemed set on marrying anyone of late, I can abandon the idea of giving it to you. Besides, it would make a thankless gift, for the cost of repairs would no doubt ruin your pockets, deep though they are. I'll get my solicitor to find a buyer for the property."

"A very sensible course," her nephew agreed. Now that the matter was settled, he rose to his feet, for he was late for an appointment at Gentleman Jack's.

"By the by, Peter, did you perchance receive an invitation to the Vyne party next week?" his aunt asked as she walked him to the door.

Prescott's dark eyes narrowed. "I did. It quite bowled me over."

"Are you attending?"

"Yes. Are you?"

"Perhaps."

"Then how would it sit if I were your escort?"

His aunt accepted his offer with genuine pleasure tinged with a modicum of guilt. And she devoutly hoped as she made her way back to her sitting room that Lavinia would not remember who had planted the notion in her pea-brain about inviting Prescott to her dreary ball.

CHAPTER TWO

Mrs. Edgewater was not alone in thinking that Lady Vyne's ball would be a penance. The hostess's younger brother, Sir Donald Whiting, echoed those sentiments, exclaiming at length about his sister's skip-brained notion. He railed so unremittingly, that his wife was at last constrained to remind him that it was of no use to complain to her. Lavinia was, after all, his sister.

Apparently unmoved by her family's consternation, Eleanor set off from Mount Street the next morning with her good friend Diana Hawthorne. A brisk wind blew as they headed over the cobblestoned streets toward Madame Fanchon's shop, bringing a ruddy colour to Eleanor's cheeks. Like that of all young ladies, her interest in fashion was keen, but she had a far more telling reason to seek out Fanchon today, for, if she really did attend her Aunt Lavinia's ball she was determined to be in her best looks.

Diana settled herself back as the tilbury bounced along. A friend from childhood, Mrs. Hawthorne suited her Christian name for she loved flowers and gardens, and possessed the sylphlike shape of a wood nymph, a resemblance augmented this morning by her choice of a sea-green muslin walking dress.

She chattered to Eleanor about the play by Mr. Richard Sheridan, which she and her husband Philip had enjoyed the previous evening, and enquired whether Eleanor had seen it as yet.

"Oh yes," Eleanor said politely, but in truth her mind was not on Drury Lane.

Diana twirled a curl of hair around a finger. "My dearest friend, you know I rely on you to tell me if I grow as prosey and as boring as dreary Mrs. Drummond Burrell."

This won a chuckle from Eleanor. The very notion of comparing the lovely Diana to the grimfaced Patroness with at least sixty years in her dish was the outside of enough.

"Now that is more the thing," Diana said. "You have been looking so Friday-faced since we left Mount Street."

"A consequence of driving in Town traffic," Eleanor said, leading her team around a particularly congested corner. "I vow it gets worse each Season with coachmen from the country and tradesmen and mere whipsters believing they are ready for the Four Horse Club."

"I don't have your skill or courage for such exercise," Diana admitted as the carriage rolled over a patch of road which boasted more than its fair share of loose cobblestones. "Now, what are you planning to get at Fanchon's? A new pelisse? A walking dress?"

"No, I thought it time I ordered a new ball gown. Something distinctive, out of the ordinary."

Diana's delicately framed eyebrows flew up. "Is there a special reason for such a purchase?" she enquired softly.

Eleanor decided to open her budget completely. Diana was after all her bosom bow. "My aunt Lavinia is giving a ball for my cousin Maria's come-out. She plans to invite Lord Prescott.''

Mrs. Hawthorne's cheerful face froze, her mouth dropped open, and she uttered a piercing shriek of surprise.

Eleanor's hand tightened on the reins as she fought to control her two greys.

"Good heavens, Di, don't shriek like that again or my team will certainly bolt," Eleanor scolded, not relishing the explanations to her father's groom about such an accident. The servant had already been put in the sulks at not accompanying her on the morning drive.

"I'm sorry," Diana said, stricken to the core. "I didn't mean to overset you or the horses, but I never thought I'd live to hear you mention that man's name again."

"Well, I shan't live at all if you keep shrieking in that demented way while I am driving," Eleanor said dampeningly.

For a few minutes Diana was silent as Eleanor concentrated on the horses, but curiosity finally got the best of her.

"Do you mean that you are seriously contemplating attending the same ball as Prescott?" she asked in her quiet way.

"I don't know yet. Papa forbade any of us to go. But if I do attend I am determined to look my best. Lord Prescott shall not think me hagged or sunk into a decline. Being so odiously arrogant, he'd undoubtedly think it's on his account."

A contemplative expression entered Mrs. Hawthorne's eyes as she gazed over at her friend. Impossible that anyone should call Eleanor hagged for she

was still highly fêted in the ton with at least three
gentlemen of Quality dangling after her. As for sink-
ing into a decline over Prescott, Diana, a truthful sort,
was not prepared to go that far, but she sometimes
thought that her friend was more melancholy than she
had been three years ago.

Diana's musing came to a premature end as Eleanor
brought the carriage expertly up to the front of Fanchon's shop. The two ladies stepped down and Eleanor
looped the reins expertly through the tether-post. Then
the friends entered the bustling establishment that was
crowded with matrons consulting one another on the
proper cloth and colour to bring out the best features
of their marriage-minded daughters.

Fanchon's assistants hurried down the aisles to do
the customers' bidding, while from the back room
Mme. Fanchon herself could be heard conversing with
someone in fluent French.

"Oh look at this, Eleanor," Diana said, laying a
gloved hand on a sketch Fanchon had left on her table. "It is very pretty and unusual."

"Pretty for a seventeen-year-old miss just emerged
from a schoolroom," Eleanor said dismissively. "But
I am not that."

"Then what of this," Diana asked, pointing to another sketch showing a very daring off-the-shoulder
gown. "You could have it done up in red silk!" she
teased.

"And be taken for some high-flyer? Do be serious.
I rely on you for help, not hindrance."

Obediently, Diana lent her assistance to the task
before them, and after a half hour the two ladies
reached agreement on a sapphire-blue satin with an
azure silk overdress. As for the style, Eleanor was in-

clined to go along with Diana's suggestion of the Grecian mode that was very much the rage.

Providentially, just as they had agreed on the cloth and the style, Fanchon herself stepped out from the back room, accompanied by a tall, statuesque blonde. The two made their way in unhurried fashion toward the door.

"Who is that lady, Mama?" a freckled young lady asked.

The matron addressed sniffed loudly. "That is no lady, my love," she replied to her daughter.

A silence fell, and the Frenchwoman herself turned, her beautiful face utterly indifferent to the insult, but when her grey eyes glanced Eleanor's way they widened slightly. Then she nodded in recognition and left the shop.

"Who is she, Mama?" the freckled girl continued into the resulting buzz of conversation.

"No one important," her mother said with exasperation. "What about this for the underdress?"

"She looks important."

"Looks can be deceiving.... She is no one you need pay attention to." The mother steered her daughter toward some bolts of cloth.

"But what is her name?"

"Oh, do stop your chattering, child!"

Eleanor could have answered the young lady's torrent of questions for the beautiful blonde Frenchwoman was Aimée Martine, a Cyprian of the highest order and the reason Eleanor had not wed Prescott three years ago.

She had known from the beginning that Prescott had kept a *chère amie*. Rare was the gentleman who did not. She had, however, expected that once they

were married that tie would be broken. She had said
as much to him during the course of their courtship,
receiving his assurances that his relationship with Aimée was only one of form and that he would give her
her congé soon.

Deeply in love with him, Eleanor believed him, until that fatal day when during an excursion to Hampton Court with Andrew she had glimpsed Prescott and
Aimée under a lime tree. From the way the Frenchwoman clung to and kissed him she knew that the affair was not over.

He had lied about breaking off the attachment, and
this Eleanor would never countenance. If he wanted
his bit of muslin, she stormed to herself, he could have
her and his ring back as well. The next day she had
dispatched her footman on his errand.

"Mademoiselle Whiting? You have an order today?"

Madame Fanchon, the genius of modistes, stood
ready to do her bidding. Eleanor quickly filled the
modiste in on her needs for the new ball gown, but
even as she submitted to the tape measure, she could
not help but think of Prescott's lovely bird of para-
dise.

FOUR HOURS LATER in her Grosvenor Square sitting
room, Aimée Martine called a halt to her posing.

"*Mon Dieu*, my back is near to killing me," she
said, rising from the Etruscan-armed sofa and
stretching her back like a cat.

"*Non, non*. You have spoiled it," Armand Saint
Jacques, the artist, said in accents of despair as he laid
down his palette. "I shall never capture the light
against your skin like that again."

"Of course, you will!" she contradicted with a rallying laugh. "You say the same thing every day. You would paint me every moment of the day until I am as stoop-shouldered as a crone. I wonder that you would ever go away if I did not send you away."

Armand put down his brushes. Flecks of gold paint dotted his dark hair. "How can I bear to go from you, Aimée, when you are my mode, my inspiration," he said simply.

In any other man the words would have sounded false, but Armand was special to Aimée, and her look was warm as she pecked him on the cheek. "*Cher* Armand. You are always so gallant, and I vow that today I can use every ounce of it." She moved behind a Chinese screen and pulled on a dressing gown over her white and nearly transparent shift.

"Why, so pensive, *cherie?*" Armand asked, cleaning his brushes with a cloth. "I notice that today your mood is not your usual gay one."

"*Oui,*" she agreed. "But it is nothing, truly. Ow, my back hurts." She pressed her hand to the throbbing muscles of her shoulder.

"*Pauvre petite,* let me," Armand said, stricken with conscience. He put down his cloth and began to massage her shoulders. "Better?"

She purred her contentment. Armand's hands worked their way down her spine.

Of all the artists who painted her Armand Saint Jacques was Aimée's particular favorite. They had met a year ago at an exhibition at Somerset House and had at once formed a bond. At times it seemed to Aimée that he was her twin spirit, so acute was he at gauging her moods. He was also a brilliant artist and as his model she responded to his desire to capture her on canvas. A pity he was so poor.

"Why are you troubled?" he asked now. "Is it this Prescott, still? How he mistreats you. I wish you would come and live with me instead of here."

Aimée pulled away. She enjoyed Prescott's patronage, and she would not listen to a word against him. In matters of love she was very loyal. "Prescott? Don't be silly. He hasn't seen me in at least a month and then it was quite by chance in the street. I think he has forgotten that I am supposed to be his mistress."

"And if that is not mistreatment of a beautiful lady, what is?" Armand demanded bluntly.

Aimée rose and paced the length of her sitting room. Her legs felt as wobbly as a newborn colt's from the posing.

"You have not answered my question, Aimée," Armand chided.

Aimée shrugged. "You and I are French. The English are different. And as one English lady pointed out to her daughter today. I am no lady."

"*Sacre bleu!* What I would have done to such a person if I had been there. Come and live with me, Aimée." He crossed the room and took her in his arms.

"Armand, please."

"I love you, Aimée, and you love me."

She dared not speak. He flung his hands up, releasing her. "I know why you will not. It is because I am not able to keep you in such clothes and in such a fine house."

"Well, yes," Aimée said frankly. She was not an avaricious creature, but she did prefer a comfortable life. With Prescott as her benefactor she need never quibble about the bills she ran up at the modiste or milliner, and her rent was always paid. She had grown up poor and never wanted to return to the days of worrying about a loaf of bread.

"You are a good friend, Armand, and you know I love you. But you cannot afford me."

"Someday I will."

"Ah well, when that day comes we shall elope, shall we not?" she teased and touched his cheek lightly with her finger. "Did I tell you I am posing for John Sebastian later this week?" she asked, changing the subject.

"I don't want you posing for Sebastian."

Aimée laughed, not entirely displeased by Armand's reaction. At her advanced age of thirty it was exhilarating to have someone like Armand in love with her. He was very handsome too, with his curly black hair falling over his eyes.

"I am not just your model," she reminded him. "And undoubtedly Sebastian will paint a landscape, and I shall probably show up as a shepherdess."

"More likely Venus," Armand muttered and turned back to his brushes.

Knowing that Armand could sulk all afternoon, Aimée deemed it a stroke of good fortune when Lord Prescott was announced a few minutes later. She hurried to greet him and the sight of the lovely Frenchwoman in the arms of her handsome patron brought Armand's session to an abrupt end.

"I don't think your painter likes me, Aimée," Prescott said, observing Armand's rapid departure with some amusement.

"He is an artist," she replied, relieved that Prescott took Armand's presence without a blink. Once he would have stormed and raged. How different it was now between them. Giving her head a little shake, she led him toward the velvet settee. "How have you been, *cheri?*"

"Well enough," he assured her, giving her hand an absentminded kiss. It was, she realized ruefully, almost a chaste salute.

"Well, you do not look up to snuff," she replied. "You look tired."

"For that you may blame my abominable luck at the card table. I was up all night at Watier's. I never had the knack of falling asleep during the day."

"You had no trouble sleeping in the day here, as I recall," she said, her hand lightly stroking his.

He smiled at the memory. "We weren't really sleeping, though, were we, Aimée?" he teased.

"Sit down and have some sherry or would you rather claret?"

"Claret will do nicely." He sank down on the small couch. "I saw some of the paintings that Armand did of you last year. They don't do your beauty justice."

She laughed. "He will be livid if you say that to him. He is very talented.

"You are turning up everywhere. I vow, I have only to look at a painting to see your face."

"It does seem that way," she agreed. "And while the outcome is always pleasant you have no idea how exhausting it is to keep perfectly still while someone paints you. And if you dare to twitch your nose because of an itch how they howl with outrage."

He laughed, and they sipped their claret in companionable silence.

"Something's different here. What is it? New wallpaper?"

"The Chinese screen," she informed him, pointing to the black lacquered screen, carved with dragons in gold.

"Very handsome."

"Armand advised me to buy it. He said that not only was it beautiful, it could be valuable some day."

"Is that so? It does give the whole room a different look. I shall have to ask his advice on any purchases I make."

"I'm sure Armand will be happy to assist you." She stroked his knee lightly, a mere feather's touch. "So how went your visit to the country?"

"Dreary," he said. "My aunt's estate is so badly neglected that it will cost her dearly to repair. So she has decided to sell it."

Aimée's ears pricked up, and she ceased caressing his knee. "How much does she want for it?"

"No price was set. Why? Are you interested in a country home? I should think this establishment would be enough."

"This is not mine but yours," she reminded him. "Or you hold the lease on it. One cannot become attached to someone else's property. It is a fatal mistake." Her words were quietly but firmly spoken.

Prescott cocked his head at her. "I never knew your feelings were so strong, Aimée."

She shrugged, her shoulders moving lightly under the dressing gown. "Some day I shall have my own home. Perhaps back in France."

"France?" This was a surprise to Prescott. "You are homesick?" he asked.

She gave a wintry smile. "London is not Paris. More claret?"

She rose to fill his glass and then sat down again next to him on the settee. He pulled her close, and encouraged her to talk about France. After ten minutes she became aware that the arm about her shoulders was growing heavy, and she glanced up. Lord Prescott was sound asleep.

CHAPTER THREE

THE STOUT, GREY-HAIRED gentleman standing in front of the pier glass appeared at first to be gazing intently at the chubby nymphs on his ceiling, but closer scrutiny revealed that Sir Donald Whiting was in fact attempting the all-important positioning of the folds of his cravat.

Drop his neck too quickly, and all would be lost. With bated breath, his valet, James, waited until finally the baronet's gaze was level in the glass.

"That will do, James."

"Very good, my lord."

Sir Donald gave his cravat a final pat. Thank Jupiter that was now a fait accompli. He was no tulip, and the tying of a creditable Mathematical always challenged his fingers. But that challenge was nothing compared to this infernal ball of Lavinia's.

Sir Donald sighed. Like most fathers blessed with a lovely, intelligent daughter, he was a trifle in awe of the Beauty he had sired. Three years ago when against his best advice she had been determined to receive the attentions of Prescott, he had warned her that she would come to grief. And when that affair ended badly she had smiled gallantly at him through tear-filled eyes and said: "Papa, you were right."

Sir Donald didn't enjoy being right. And he didn't enjoy his daughter's unhappiness. He would have gladly strangled his sister Lavinia for being such a ninnyhammer as to invite them to the same ball as Prescott.

"And I still do not see why we must go. Ball for Maria, indeed," he complained to his wife when he looked in on her in her dressing room.

"We must go because Eleanor is going," Lady Constance said calmly, applying a touch of French perfume to each pulse point on her wrists.

"And why does Eleanor wish to go?" Sir Donald asked uneasily. "You don't think she's going to fling another piece of muslin in Prescott's face, do you?"

Lady Constance, her hand hovering now over a rouge pot, halted as she seriously considered her husband's words.

"Heavens, I don't think she'd do such a thing. But then I never dreamed she'd do it three years ago either."

"And why the devil must we take Harry Addison with us?"

"Because he has asked to be Eleanor's escort, and she consented. Harry is a pleasant boy."

Lady Constance rose from her seat in front of her looking glass, affording Sir Donald a look at a shimmery green satin gown. With her hair dressed in a becoming Sappho she resembled one of those sea creatures that had bewitched Ulysses of old and he promptly told her so.

"Donald, I vow, you are a romantic," she said, kissing him lightly and searching for her fan. "Now let me see if Eleanor is ready."

Thanks to the concerted efforts of Madame Fanchon, her own maid, Matilde, and herself, Eleanor was indeed ready and, as her parents were quick to point out, in her best looks. Her deep blue ball gown was cut discreetly low, showing just a hint of bosom, further enhanced by an exquisite sapphire necklace.

And if that didn't make Prescott rue the day he was born, nothing would, Sir Donald thought with justifiable paternal pride.

"Well, Papa, will I do?" Eleanor asked.

"My word, yes, my dear," Sir Donald said. "Now, let's be off to this infernal ball."

Pausing only to take a last look in the mirror, Eleanor picked up her skirts and swept out of the room with her father and mother. As she descended the Adam stairs, Mr. Harry Addison, her escort, came forward. Handsome Harry, the quizzes called him, and so he was, his blonde, burnished locks cut in the fashionable Brutus and his tall, lanky frame dressed in the black, swallow-tailed coat and knee breeches that constituted evening dress for gentlemen of the ton.

Harry smiled as Eleanor approached, his blue eyes a trifle less vacuous than usual.

"Eleanor, first rate, I'd say. You look beautiful."

"Thank you, Harry," she said, as he kissed her hand.

The two made a striking pair. Sir Donald had been inclined to dismiss Harry Addison as nothing more than an Adonis. But as he regarded the handsome couple before him he could not help wondering who would accompany Prescott to Lavinia's ball.

At that very moment Lord Prescott's town carriage drew to a stop in front of the Hill Street residence of Lady Vyne. His lordship emerged, looking despite the presence of a dozen dandies and tulips quite the most elegant gentleman present. Certainly, his shoulders filled his swallow-tailed coat to perfection and his intricate cravat a l'Oriental would doubtless provoke envious comments from the younger set.

Turning, he held a hand out to his companion, dressed to the nines this evening in a cream-coloured spider gauze and an ostrich-feathered hat.

"Well, Aunt Judith, ready to waltz?"

"Waltz?" She gave a cackle of laughter. "You absurd boy. All I wish to do is to find a comfortable chair and sit there for the evening."

"If such is the case why did you agree to come?" he drawled, as they joined the throng now entering the Vyne establishment.

Mrs. Edgewater fanned herself lightly with an ivory fan. "I had a feeling this would be an interesting evening," she said obliquely.

Lady Vyne had spared no expense for the ball, as evidenced by the number of servants scurrying everywhere as well as by the huge bower of flowers her guests were obliged to pass through as they made their way up the staircase.

Was it her imagination, Mrs. Edgewater wondered, or did her nephew seem to be searching the faces of the guests for one in particular?

Looking regal in a tiara trimmed in emeralds and diamonds and an elaborate gown, Lady Vyne received Prescott with an excess of enthusiasm. She prattled on to him about the great honour he did her by gracing her ball.

Then she brought forward young Maria Whiting. "My niece, my lord. Maria, this is Lord Prescott and Mrs. Edgewater."

Maria dipped a curtsey, looking half-frightened to death. Attired in a pink satin gown, she was so newly emerged from the schoolroom as to be in awe of everything and anything she saw around her. Indeed she was nearly agog at the beautifully gowned ladies swirling past on the arms of the handsome gentlemen.

A pretty little thing, Prescott decided as he smiled at her, in the Immaculata style with blonde hair and blues eyes, but hardly the diamond of the first water that Eleanor was.

"Lord Prescott, Maria has been practising the waltz faithfully for a week. I told her that you were the most expert waltzer in the ton."

"Kind words, Lady Vyne. But my knee has been troubling me of late. Old war injury," he said, and passed on before Maria's imaginary skills as a nurse could be conjured up.

"What will you do when Lavinia finds out you were never in battle during the war?" Mrs. Edgewater chuckled.

"I will enlist, and make good the cheat," he said.

Hearing her name called by one of her cronies, Mrs. Edgewater temporarily deserted her nephew and went off to join them, leaving him to venture alone into the ballroom armed only with his quizzing glass.

With a sigh, he took out his snuff box. Why the devil *had* he come? He was too old for balls and routs. The laughter and chattering voices did not enthrall him as they did Miss Maria Whiting but instead reminded him of Bedlam. A distinct sense of ennui set in as Prescott dipped his fingers into his snuff mixture. He'd seen it all before countless times. Except for one person.

"She's not here yet," Mrs. Edgewater said, reappearing at his side.

"Of whom are you speaking?" he enquired, taking a pinch of snuff.

"Do stop this stupid dissembling," his aunt remarked acidly. "We both know you are looking for Eleanor Whiting. Her brother Andrew is here with his young wife and I took the liberty of speaking with them."

"Which is Andrew's wife?" Prescott asked, his interest piqued by his aunt's information. He had always liked Eleanor's brother, a scientifically inclined fellow with a love of sport which rivalled his own.

"The little blonde," Mrs. Edgewater said now.

"Ah yes," Prescott said, his glance settling on the smiling lady standing next to Andrew.

"Has a weakness for gaming."

Prescott lifted a brow.

"Really, Aunt Judith! You could deduce all that from only five minutes conversation with the pair? You put me in the liveliest dread of what you would deduce after an hour with anyone."

His aunt laughed. "People make the mistake of underestimating an old woman like me. I advise you not to. And as for young Julia, I met a creditor of hers yesterday whose tongue does run on wheels."

"Does Andrew know?"

"Not yet. According to the on-dits, young Julia is trying to keep from sitting down to cards, but old habits die hard."

Indeed they did, Prescott agreed as an old habit by the name of Eleanor Whiting entered the ballroom on the arm of Harry Addison. Seeing the two together brought home the inevitable fact that she might soon marry him.

"She's as beautiful as ever," Mrs. Edgewater said, watching her nephew closely.

"I disagree, Aunt," he said, polishing his quizzing glass.

"You detect a flaw?" she asked, astounded.

"None whatsoever. You mistake the matter. She's even more beautiful than I can recall."

Eleanor had never lacked for style, Prescott thought, as she swept into the ballroom in a blue gown that showed her tiny waist to perfection. Her sapphire-and-diamond necklace sparkled in the light cast by the chandelier. A present from Addison? he wondered, unaware that he was frowning furiously.

"The handsomest pair in the room," Mrs. Edgewater said, a comment that was reiterated by many during the course of the evening. Prescott put down his glass, nettled at seeing Eleanor looking so well. As though, he thought bitterly, she had never lost a night's sleep over him.

Eleanor was acutely conscious of Prescott's presence. How could she be otherwise, since Lady Vyne had babbled about it in the receiving line. The air in the ballroom seemed electric as every eye watched as she and Harry strolled over to Andrew and Julia. After a few minutes she felt sufficiently emboldened to cast an oblique eye of her own about the ballroom, her gaze flitting from face to face until they hit upon one in particular.

Even though they were separated by the full length of the room Eleanor felt a jolt down to her knees. She would not have been surprised had she fallen from the sheer force of Prescott's gaze.

"Dance with me," Andrew whispered in her ear.

"I don't know if I can make it through the waltz,"
she confessed, but he overrode her protests and led her
out. A series of dizzying spins left her breathless and
brought colour back to her cheeks.

"That's better. You looked much too pale when you
saw Prescott."

"Do you think anyone else noticed I was a trifle
undone?" she asked, conscious of Andrew's sympa-
thetic gaze.

"Julia may have, but I don't think your handsome
beau did."

She laughed in genuine amusement. Harry had
many virtues but being needlewitted was not amongst
them.

"Prescott has been looking for you ever since he
arrived," Andrew went on.

"The better to examine me with that odious quizzing glass of his," she said, her lip curling slightly.
"Searching for every detectable flaw."

"Then he'd search in vain," Andrew said. "Now,
smile. We can't have him thinking that he has dis-
comforted you, can we?"

"No indeed," she agreed, giving him a dazzling
smile.

"Not that dazzling," he grumbled. "I'm just your
brother. Save that for Harry Addison."

She laughed again. The waltz and Andrew had done
the thing. Her mood had turned. She would not be
such a henwit as to fall to pieces if Prescott ventured
a word to her. But would he? For most of the ball he
kept his distance, standing next to Mrs. Edgewater and
content enough to observe the twirling couples with
that quizzing glass.

This did not prevent some of the bolder ladies from setting their caps at him, coming over to speak to him under the guise of exchanging a word with his aunt.

"Eleanor, I say, Eleanor," Harry Addison's voice of mild complaint roused her from her reverie some time later, as they danced.

"Oh Harry, pray forgive me. I was just trying to think of the name of that milliner that Diana had recommended to me the other day. What were you saying?"

Outwardly Prescott betrayed little emotion at the sight of Eleanor and Addison together, but his aunt, sitting in the chair next to him, observed the muscle quivering in his jaw, a tension he attempted to mask by a vigorous polishing of his quizzing glass.

Someone ought to wrap that odious glass about his neck, Eleanor thought as she danced past with Harry and unleashed a dazzling smile on her handsome partner. Mr. Addison was at best a merely adequate dancer, since this was a skill that necessitated his moving various parts of his body at the same time, and he was a trifle overcome by Eleanor's smile, so much so that he lost track of the count in the music and stepped firmly on her foot.

"Oh . . ." she exclaimed.

"Having difficulty, Mr. Addison?" Mrs. Edgewater enquired, and Eleanor looked up in acute mortification to see Prescott and his aunt sitting within a foot of them, Prescott still holding the odious quizzing glass to one eye.

"Well, just a trifle," Harry explained to Mrs. Edgewater. "Stepped on Miss Whiting's shoe. Hope there's been no irreparable damage."

"Yes, a rather ticklish business, dancing," Prescott agreed. "Having to move one's feet at the same time that one has to keep count to the music."

"Perhaps you shouldn't dance any more, but sit," Mrs. Edgewater said as Prescott indicated the vacant chair next to his aunt.

Having no choice in the matter, Eleanor sat down.

"Mr. Addison, might a decrepit old lady prevail upon you for a glass of champagne?" Mrs. Edgewater enquired, and Harry glad of something useful to do, went off to fetch a glass for her and Eleanor.

"Harry Addison might be an Adonis, but if I were you I'd not dance with him again," Prescott said after Harry had gone.

"I don't recall asking your advice, my lord," Eleanor said, lifting her chin. The three years had not changed his insufferable manners.

"No, you didn't," he agreed. "But you should listen to what your feet are telling you about partnering Harry." He bent over to examine one of her shoes.

"Why don't you put that odious glass away?" she asked. "I vow, you make anyone feel like a piece of cattle."

"Have I used it that much?" he asked, letting it fall.

She flushed, aware that now he knew she had been observing him.

"Well, I don't need a glass to see that Harry Addison is coming back with the champagne," Mrs. Edgewater said rising to the occasion. "I shall intercept him and allow you two to have a comfortable cose."

A comfortable cose. Eleanor dreaded the thought of any such thing with Prescott. But it was too late, for

Mrs. Edgewater was indeed plunging into the middle of the crowd, headed toward Harry.

"Well, Miss Whiting, would you as lief have our comfortable cose here or on the dance floor?" Prescott enquired, his brown eyes holding the mocking glint that was so familiar to her.

"I'd rather not speak to you at all, my lord," she declared, not caring if her words sounded uncivil.

"What a pity. After all the shifts you have been put to?"

Eleanor stiffened. "Shifts? What do you mean?"

He stroked his chin and glanced down at her. The years had not changed her ethereal loveliness. "I suspect you had to do a good deal of maneuvering to get your aunt to invite me to this ball. And as for choosing that precise moment in your dance with Harry to scold him about his footwork..." One eyebrow rose quizzingly. "But you needn't worry, Miss Whiting, I am ready to accept your attempt at peacemaking."

"My attempt?" Eleanor could not believe her ears. "I assure you, my lord, my aunt's ball and her guest list were none of my concern."

The mockery in his eyes grew more pronounced, nearly tempting her to box his ears. Before she allowed herself to do so she turned on heel and marched off.

Knowing full well that she was flushed and out of sorts, she left the ballroom and went out onto a nearby terrace to inhale some fresh air. She needed to think. Her temples throbbed. Lord Prescott was still the same arrogant man he'd been three years ago.

"Eleanor, I thought I saw you come out here." Harry Addison stepped out onto the terrace a few minutes later. "Do you want your glass of champagne?"

"Yes, of course," she said, taking it and draining it all in one gulp.

"Good heavens, you were thirsty, weren't you?" he said. "And you are flushed too. How is your foot?"

"My foot? Oh, it is much better. You needn't concern yourself with it."

"But I must. Such a lummox I am," he said, peering down at it.

Was every gentleman tonight determined to look at her shoes, Eleanor wondered as she extended her foot and bent her head.

As she did so she felt a trifle dizzy, as though the champagne she had drunk had suddenly rushed to her head. Her surroundings swam before her eyes, and she felt herself fall.

"Good heavens, Eleanor," Harry Addison exclaimed as she pitched forward into his arms, just as Lord Prescott stepped out onto the terrace.

The sight of Eleanor locked in what looked to be a lover's embrace brought an immediate cessation to Prescott's need for air. At once he retraced his steps into the ballroom, thinking as he did so that perhaps the Adonis had more than good looks to offer Miss Whiting. Certainly she had never swooned from one of his kisses three years ago.

CHAPTER FOUR

THE SILHOUETTE in the early-morning light displayed a generously curved figure in a white chemise. Aimée Martine was at the peak of her womanhood, and knew it.

From the window she glanced over at the bed where Lord Prescott lay sleeping. When he had descended on Grosvenor Square last night at midnight, she had hoped her three years of patience had been rewarded. But after a few brandies he had fallen asleep, leaving her to undress him and put him to bed.

She was acting more as a nursemaid to him these days than a lover. And it must end. She was too proud to continue playing the patient mistress to a man who never sought her kisses or caresses any more.

Prescott rolled over in bed and groaned.

"Bonjour," she greeted him.

"Good morning," he returned, rubbing his eyes with his fists. "You look lovely today, *chérie.*"

His compliment, however sincere, left her sadly flat. It wasn't that Prescott was saying the wrong things, but that the words lacked feeling.

"You have seen her, haven't you? Eleanor Whiting."

He paused and shot her a quick look. "She was at a ball last night. Why do you ask?"

"You called her name out in your sleep last night."

Prescott felt a pang of guilt. "Deuced sorry about that, Aimée."

"*Ce n'est rien.* I'd rather you call it out when you are asleep then when we make love." Her eyes met his. "But then we haven't made love in almost three years."

"That can be changed," he said, kissing her deeply. For a moment she relaxed in his arms. It was almost like before, but then she broke away in tears.

"What's the matter? I thought you wanted . . ."

"I want you to make love to me!" Aimée exclaimed. "Not to her. And that's what you are doing when you kiss me. I sense it."

"Females!" he complained, rising from the bed and reaching for his clothes. "You get on your high ropes because I don't make love to you, and when I do—!"

Aimée sat on the bed, watching him button his shirt. "I saw her the other day at Fanchon's. I almost told you about it. But then, what female likes to bring a rival to her lover's mind?"

"She is not your rival," he said slowly.

"No," she agreed, watching him in the looking glass. But she was once. When Prescott informed her three years ago that their relationship was over, Aimée was put into a flame, refusing to believe it possible. That he might marry she had long ago come to accept as inevitable, but that he would end their longtime relationship was unacceptable.

She had taken steps to see this Eleanor Whiting for herself. She was a Beauty, right and proper, but there was more to her than that. The hazel eyes shone with intelligence and laughter, and for the first time in her life Aimée felt frightened of another woman. This one might indeed be her equal.

She had arranged to meet Prescott for one last time at Hampton Court on a day when she knew Eleanor would be present. Inventing a tale about her dying father in France, she collapsed into Prescott's arms. He comforted her as she knew he would, for he was not a heartless ogre.

Her ploy had succeeded. Eleanor had broken off the impending nuptials the very next day, and in such a fashion as to infuriate Prescott. Aimée had rejoiced in her victory. Prescott might marry another lady some time later but for now they could continue their liaison. But oddly enough the bond between them changed, and although he spoke contemptuously of stepping in parson's mousetrap and continued to support her in style, their relationship too had cooled. Eleanor Whiting had won.

At the precise moment when Prescott was leaving Aimée's house on Grosvenor Square, Eleanor, in a burgundy riding habit was driving her tilbury down the Strand toward the City, headed for her morning's appointment with her publisher, Mr. Fischer.

Her head throbbed slightly, a result of the glass of champagne she had drunk the night before. Was this what gentlemen complained of when they were foxed? she wondered. And it was a very good thing she had had only the one glass of champagne for if she had consumed more her head would be aching even more violently than it was.

Thinking of the ball brought Prescott to mind. He hadn't changed. Her hands tightened on the reins of the greys, which were champing at the bit to run. Behind her, the groom clucked his tongue in warning. And his lordship wasn't half as handsome as Harry, she thought slackening her grip.

Harry. She felt a moment's discomfiture recalling how she had toppled at his feet on the terrace. Fortunately she had recovered almost at once. And no one except Harry had seen her. If Prescott had witnessed such a sight he would no doubt have roared with laughter.

Ten minutes later, seated in a hard-backed chair, she watched Mr. Fischer fiddle with his gold spectacles. Her manuscript lay between them on his cluttered desk.

"Well, Mr. Fischer, what do you think?" she asked.

The publisher rubbed his slightly balding pate. "Well, Miss Whiting, I can see that you spent considerable time and thought on the new poems."

"Yes. After all, you were the one who urged me to write another volume of verse."

"Yes, I know, your first efforts were such a resounding success. All that emotion, even, begging your pardon, passion. Some were hard put to believe that a lady of Quality could pen them."

"That is why I chose anonymity," Eleanor said with a smile. "But what of my new work? When will you be bringing it out?"

The publisher coughed. "Well, actually, Miss Whiting, I thought I would give you a chance to revise a few of the poems."

"Which ones?"

"Well, perhaps those in the beginning and in the end. And one mustn't forget the middle, either."

"The beginning, the middle and the end?" Eleanor asked, astounded. "Good heavens, Mr. Fischer, are you telling me that you don't think my manuscript worth publishing at all?"

"I just thought that perhaps if we waited and you wrote a little more, we could improve the manuscript," he said.

"I see," Eleanor said not terribly surprised by his criticism. She herself had found the poems far inferior to her first volume, but had still thought it best to seek Mr. Fischer's opinion. How vexatious that it was the same as hers.

"You mustn't spare me, Mr. Fischer. You think my verse horrid, do you not?"

"Oh, Miss Whiting, I should not go that far. If you could just work on it more, I'm sure—"

"Your assurances are not necessary," Eleanor said, tucking the manuscript under one arm.

"Where are you going?"

"To the Serpentine."

Mr. Fischer's Adam's apple bobbed up and down in a convulsive manner. "Miss Whiting, you mustn't throw yourself in the lake!" he exclaimed.

Eleanor laughed, her ready sense of the ridiculous delighting in the publisher's melodramatic imagination.

"Hardly, sir," she said, controlling a quivering lip. "I intend to throw the manuscript in instead."

Feeling much better now that she had adopted a course of action, she descended the stairs and prepared to climb into her carriage, a plan that she delayed when she noticed her sister-in-law Julia hurriedly walking down the street.

"Julia!" Eleanor called out.

Dressed in a dove-grey morning dress, Mrs. Whiting turned. Surprise and marked anxiety showed on her pretty face as she neared the carriage.

"Eleanor, what are you doing here?"

"I had a visit with my publisher who tells me that the Muse has deserted me."

"Oh no," Julia said with quick sympathy. "How disappointing for you. What will you do?"

"I'm going to throw the manuscript into the Serpentine. Where were you bound for, looking so serious?"

Julia toyed with the ribbon of her chip hat. She resembled a Dresden china doll in it. "I was on my way home."

Eleanor's eyes scanned the vicinity. "Where is your carriage?"

"I came in a hack."

"Well, let me take you home," Eleanor suggested. "If you don't mind a visit to the Serpentine first."

"The Serpentine. You weren't serious about throwing your manuscript in, were you?" Julia asked as she settled into the carriage.

"Indeed I was," Eleanor averred, giving her greys their head. "Does Andrew know you are racketing about the City at this hour?" And didn't you take your maid?"

"No," Julia said to both questions, hanging on for dear life as the carriage swayed round a corner. "And please, Eleanor, you must not tell Andrew. Please, promise you won't tell him."

Her stricken appeal made not a jot of sense to Eleanor. Andrew was no blackguard, but Julia appeared in such a quake lest he learn of her visit to the City. And just what was Julia doing in the City, alone?

"I shall tell you if your promise not to tell Andrew," Julia said.

"Very well. I promise."

"I was paying a visit to Messrs. Smith and King."

"The moneylenders? Julia! Whatever for? Don't tell me that Andrew has fallen into the briars?"

"No. Not Andrew, Eleanor, me!" Julia said and burst into tears.

Owing to the difficulty in driving a carriage while supporting a vaporish companion, Eleanor implored her sister-in-law to desist in her tears.

"For I shall probably run into that same coachman who was just screaming at me minutes ago. And the groom will tell Papa who is bound to roast me."

Julia choked on a laugh.

"There, that is much better, goose," Eleanor said, reaching her hand out to comfort her tearful companion. "Now do wait until I have reached the Park and can pull over in absolute safety and away from the prying eyes of the quizzes and you shall tell me exactly what has put you out of curl."

To her surprise Julia did hold her tongue until they left the tilbury and the groom safely parked near the Serpentine. She did not begin to speak until Eleanor, true to her promise, had thrown the pages of her manuscript into the lake.

"Aren't you the least bit sorry about your poems?" Julia asked, climbing down the slope of the lake after her.

"No, actually, it is a great relief to me. I wrote the poems just to keep myself busy. Now then—" she turned briskly to Julia "—why on earth have you applied to the moneylenders if you are short of funds? You should have come to me."

"Oh, Eleanor, how could I?" Julia asked, wringing her hands. "You are Andrew's sister. And anyway, I don't think you could lend me the sum I need."

"How much did you borrow from Messrs. Smith and King?"

"Ten thousand pounds."

"Julia! Why do you need so much money?"

"Well about five thousand is owed to my banker, Mr. Child, plus interest of course. And then one thousand is owed to Lord Randall and another two thousand to Lord Nunn. I do think that is all, but I may have forgotten someone," she concluded naively.

"But how do you mean to pay the moneylenders back?" Eleanor asked, her mind making these rapid computations. "For they do need to be paid back, you realize."

"Oh yes. I shall have the money for them. I'm quite assured that in time my luck will change. I am very lucky at the card tables. Everyone says so. Why Lord Randall said he'd rarely seen a female play her cards so well."

"Was that before or after you lost to him?" Eleanor asked sceptically.

"I can't remember," Julia said, her forehead furrowed in thought.

"I still can't believe that you have lost so much in only one year's time."

Julia hung her head. "Actually, Eleanor, some debts occurred before I married Andrew."

"But why didn't you tell him so he could discharge them?"

Julia's cheeks turned quite pink. "How could I? He thinks I'm his angel. And I never expected to lose. I'm sure that if I could just get enough money to pay off everyone, I would never touch another set of cards in

my life. But I don't have enough to do that and neither does Andrew.''

Of this fact Eleanor was only too aware. Although
no pauper Andrew would find a loan of ten thousand
difficult to repay.

"You should have come to me," she said now. "I
would have given you some of the money. Not all, of
course, because I don't have all of it."

Julia pressed her hand. "Oh, Eleanor, you are kind
to say that. But do consider. Your own money is han-
dled by your father. And were you to ask for anything over two hundred pounds I'm sure he would
demand an accounting."

This, Eleanor was bound to admit, was only too
true. Although generous to a fault her father would be
bound to question any large request.

"And I couldn't apply to your father myself," Julia said. "Not when he seemed to think that Andrew
had made a wonderful match when he married me
despite my lack of a dowry. I hate to disappoint
them."

Eleanor murmured sympathetically, but she knew
it would take more than sympathy to get Julia out of
her fix. She promised to say nothing to Andrew or her
parents, but she would keep her wits about her and
dissuade Julia from her habit in the card room.

She returned Julia to Cavendish Square, and then
drove on to Mount Street where she found her Aunt
Lavinia still reliving Maria's triumphs of the night before.

"She had Lord Merriville and Mr. Thurston dangling after her," Lady Vyne said with some relish,
sparking a flutter of protests from Maria in the cor-

ner. "One has those estates in Kent and the other is almost as rich as Golden Ball."

"You forget that one is afflicted with gout and the other with dyspepsia," Lady Constance said dampeningly. "And they both have at least fifty years in their dish. You can't be serious about them for little Maria."

"Maturity has it advantages for a husband," Lady Vyne said. "Of course it is early days yet. Edward Cassidy sent her a bouquet of roses, and Lord Tribbet invited her to ride in the Park. Even Prescott said she had the most enchanting smile of any female he had ever met, and she has gotten vouchers for Almack's!"

"Indeed?" Lady Con said, impressed despite herself with these tangible proofs of Maria's success. Recalled to the necessity of fitting Maria out for her appearance at Almack's, Lady Lavinia then drew her visit to a close, explaining that she must take her charge off to the glover. She left Lady Constance to return to her enjoyment of the *Morning Post* and Eleanor to ponder the fate of dear, sweet, goosish Julia.

SHE CAME TO NO definite conclusions but to her relief Julia seemed to eschew the card rooms at the entertainments of the the next week. Indeed when she entered the Assembly Rooms of Almack's on King Street the following Wednesday evening Julia looked her usual cheerful self in a rose-coloured silk with a beaming, devoted Andrew at her side, the pair making, as Lady Jersey observed to Lady Sefton, a veritable advertisement for the happily married state.

But just how long would that happy marriage endure with Julia's mounting debts? Eleanor wondered.

Lady Vyne bustled about the small but crowded Assembly Rooms, pleased that Maria had five suitors dangling after her, including the august Lord Prescott.

"Lady Sefton told me that his lordship rarely frequents Almack's" Lavinia said gleefully to Eleanor. "And that means he is fixing his interest in Maria. Watch for yourself."

"Heaven, I shall do no such thing," Eleanor replied, aghast at the idea of ogling Prescott while he was ogling a chit like Maria. She excused herself and went into the refreshment rooms, hoping that tonight they would be served something other than stale cakes and sour lemonade.

"Sampling the treats available this evening?" a voice asked Eleanor five minutes later as she stood contemplating the cakes.

Prescott stood next to her, his quizzing glass to his eye.

"I assure you I was using the quizzing glass to observe the cakes and not you, for I know your intense dislike of it. What think you of that lemon cake?"

"I have sampled it and found it hard as Gibraltar is rumoured to be."

He smiled. "You might think the Patronesses would order some palatable refreshments."

"They probably think the guests are more concerned about making a splendid match than about eating."

"Quite true, but even lovers must sustain themselves," he said, picking up a plate. "Your cousin granted me the privilege of bringing her some suitable refreshment,'' he explained.

"Oh.'' *Maria, of course,* she thought.

"Perhaps you could assist me,'' he turned to her. "You must know her partialities.''

"Indeed, our acquaintance is short though we are related. And I think Maria will be pleased whatever you bring her.''

"Even a stale cake.''

"From you, she must think it the sweetest ambrosia,'' Eleanor said scornfully. But to her chagrin, Prescott received her words with such unaffected good humour, thanking her so politely for the charming compliment that she was obliged to leave the refreshment room lest she give in to the real temptation to box his ears.

No sooner had she stepped back into the ballroom than she saw Andrew striding purposefully toward her. She also saw Julia's anxious face a few yards away before her sister-in-law disappeared into the thick of the crowd.

"Eleanor, I must have a word with you,'' Andrew said.

"By all means, Andrew,'' she agreed, wondering if Julia had confessed all to her brother.

"It's about Prescott.''

"Prescott!'' she exclaimed, just as his lordship himself was passing, carrying a glass of lemonade for Maria. Although he did not look her way it was obvious that he had overheard and Eleanor's cheeks burned.

"Oh, Andrew, see what you've made me do,'' she declared. "He will think that I have nothing better to do than to prattle about him at balls.''

"I beg pardon, Eleanor. Didn't mean to set you off. But I had wanted to speak to him about his aunt's country estate. I've been in the mind to buy a country home."

"Really?" Eleanor asked, mentally computing the cost of such a purchase and adding it to the already large amount of money Julia owed.

"I wanted to make sure that the hostilities were over between the two of you. Wouldn't wish to offend you, Eleanor."

"Oh, heavens, Andrew. Of course you won't offend me. Besides, the estate isn't his. It's his aunt's, and dear Mrs. Edgewater has always been quite civil to me even when what you call the hostilities were on."

"Good," Andrew beamed. "By the by, I saw Papa at White's this morning. He was attempting to hide from Harry Addison who has been trying to speak to him on a matter of mutual interest."

Eleanor turned nearly as white as her silver satin gown. "Oh heavens, he didn't, did he?"

"No, Papa put him off for the time being, but I greatly fear that your suitor is about to declare himself."

"I had hoped he wouldn't talk to Papa. That always makes it seem so serious."

"I think the matter is serious for Harry," Andrew said with a smile. "But I thought I'd drop a word in your ear."

"Thanks for the warning."

"You'd do the same for me if you saw trouble coming my way," Andrew said, giving her a peck on the cheek and making Eleanor feel like the worst of sisters.

CHAPTER FIVE

JULIA WHITING STARED down bleakly at the cards in her hands. Why had she even sat down in the card room?

"It appears that you are the winner, my lord," she said, feigning indifference as she tossed the cards onto the green baize table. She hid a delicate yawn. "Lud, but I'm fatigued. You'll forgive me if I excuse myself?"

"Of course, Mrs. Whiting," Lord Foxworth said. His heavy jowls swung as he smiled. "But there is the small matter of the thousand pounds you've lost."

Julia forced a laugh as she gathered the folds of her rose-coloured gown. "To be sure, Lord Foxworth. But I don't carry such enormous sums on my person. You will allow me to send it to you at my disposal?"

"Of course," Lord Foxworth said. "I shall be leaving London on Friday for a sojourn in the country, so I trust the money will reach me by then."

"By Friday at the latest," Julia agreed, picking up her fan and reticule and walking away on trembling legs. Why had she been so doltish as to sit down with Foxworth? He never played for chicken stakes.

Her heart caught in her throat just then as she glimpsed her tall, handsome husband waiting for her. He was the dearest, most wonderful person in the world. She had thought it an air dream when he had started to court her two years ago. Blinking back tears, she turned abruptly and almost collided with Lord Prescott.

"Mrs. Whiting, I do beg your pardon," he said, looking down from his loftier position and catching Julia as she stumbled.

"Oh, Lord Prescott, pray excuse me. Your cravat—is it ruined?" she asked.

He flicked a negligent glance down at the labour of love that was the Tróne d'Amour. "Nothing to signify, I assure you," he said, though it would have greatly signified to his valet. "I fear our collision may have put you out of curl. You are looking quite faint. May I procure you a glass of champagne? The lemonade here is far too sour."

She managed a valiant smile. "No thank you, my lord."

"Julia, there you are," Andrew said, coming up at last.

"How now, Andrew. Did you finally remember that you had a wife?" Prescott quizzed him. "Or is this the latest rage in London, to treat a young wife so absentminded? If I had a wife half as pretty as yours I would be dancing with her," he said gallantly.

Andrew fell in with Prescott's suggestion and led Julia out. His lordship watched them with an abstracted look before making his way unerringly to the card room.

In the warm arms of her husband Julia felt she was the greatest wretch in Christendom. Once the swirl of music and laughter would have rendered her giddy, but now all she could think of was how she would repay Lord Foxworth his thousand pounds. It took all her concentration to listen to Andrew, who was telling her about the Edgewater estate.

"Why do you want to look at it?" she asked.

He chuckled. "Dearest, haven't you been attending to me? I want to buy it."

"Buy it?" she squeaked, wholly astonished at such an undertaking. The cost of such a purchase plus her own debts would reduce them to penury.

"I'll have to look at it first, that goes without question. Prescott says it's fallen into disrepair. All the same I should like to buy it or something quite like it."

"But why? We have the town residence, and if we desire to go to the country we are always welcome at your father's."

"You know how it is at Thirkle with Papa and Mama in residence and usually Eleanor as well. I want a place, just for the two of us. It needn't be very grand or in tip-top shape. I would be satisfied even with some old and fusty place."

"Like a dungeon?" Julia asked gloomily.

"What? A dungeon?" Andrew laughed. "You are a minx."

Across the ballroom Eleanor was dancing, but not with Harry Addison. She had made a valiant attempt to keep her suitor at bay ever since Andrew had divulged Harry's intentions.

Eleanor had another reason for keeping out of Harry's way, for she was assisting Maria, who was perplexed at what to do with all her admirers. She had already drunk enough glasses of sour lemonade to pucker up her pretty little mouth, and it was impossible to stand up with all of them during one evening, so Eleanor danced with several of them, promising to relay their praises to her cousin's ear.

At the moment her partner was Edward Cassidy, the young gentleman who had so won Lady Vyne's good opinion. And indeed, Eleanor thought, glancing up at the strikingly fair young man, he seemed quite a good specimen with his open, unaffected manner.

She saw his distraction as his gaze wandered to their right where Maria danced with another admirer.

"Maria is very pretty, isn't she?" Eleanor said.

"I beg your pardon," he said instantly, flushing.

"Don't be," she gave him a forgiving smile. "You can't help it if your heart is elsewhere. Maria is very lucky to have won such a devoted suitor in only a se'ennight."

Mr. Cassidy emitted a rueful laugh. "I vow, Miss Whiting, I can scarcely credit it. Never thought I was the type for parson's mousetrap, but look at me. I'd marry her tomorrow if she'd say yes."

"Maria is very young and cannot know her own mind after so short an acquaintance. You'd best be patient."

"I just hope she doesn't fall prey to a scoundrel or fortune hunter."

Eleanor laughed. *Fortune hunters, indeed.* She did not know all the details of Maria's dowry, but Maria was no heiress. How peculiar that Edward would think this, and how did such a tale get about?

"From Lavinia, that goosecap," Lady Constance said in accents of despair when Eleanor put the question to her after her dance with Mr. Cassidy. "She has spread the word throughout London that Maria is an heiress. How she thinks to fool anyone with that Banbury tale I don't know. But she means to marry her off quickly before the cheat is discovered."

"And you allowed Aunt to do such a thing? Mama!"

Lady Constance flipped open her fan with disdain. "Good heavens, Eleanor, I didn't know until this evening what was afoot. I did tell Lavinia she was tempting fate. But she has never listened to me about anything."

"We shall just have to hope that Maria accepts a suitor who does not lack for money himself and who is genuinely in love with her."

"Speaking of lovesick and well-pursed swains," Lady Constance drawled, "I see Harry Addison coming this way, wearing a most determined look on his handsome face. It makes him appear rather less a mooncalf than usual. How long do you expect to fob him off?"

"As long as I can," replied her daughter, retreating to Maria's corner of the room. Maria was delighted to see her cousin again.

"I accepted Lord Randall's invitation to dance but then forgot that Lord Prescott had invited me earlier. Would you dance with him, please, Eleanor?"

Eleanor could not avoid glancing over at Prescott, who cocked one eyebrow imperiously at her as he stood talking with Randall, a veritable dandy in a violet-hued cravat.

"But of course, Maria," she said sweetly, accompanying her relation over to the two gentlemen.

"Eleanor has consented to help me out of this coil," Maria explained.

"Once Maria explained her predicament, I was glad to oblige." She favoured Prescott with a particularly sweet smile and saw the expression in his eyes darken as she turned to Lord Randall. "My lord, I should be happy to dance with you."

Lord Randall's own eyes bulged for a moment. "Oh, should you?" he asked, looking stricken. "I mean, yes, of course, Miss Whiting. Most honoured to have the opportunity to dance with you," he babbled before Eleanor took him by the hand and led him off.

Whatever pleasure she had received from tweaking Prescott's nose disappeared in the confusion of having to dance with Randall, who moved like a puppet with all four of his limbs marching to a different beat, while Lord Prescott glided effortlessly by with Maria in his arms.

Mercifully the dance ended, but before she had time even to pretend to thank Randall for it, Harry Addison swept up to claim her and led her toward a private antechamber.

"Good heavens, Harry!" she said, taken aback by such signs of masterful behaviour from her handsome beau. "What are you doing?"

"I'm trying to have a private word with you," he declared, running his fingers through his curly locks. "I vow, Eleanor, I've never had such an evening. Dancing with first one schoolroom miss and then another. And their mothers prattling on to me about their accomplishments. I want to talk to you, not some accomplished female."

"Now that's a left-handed compliment if I ever heard one," Eleanor teased.

The irritation vanished from his face to be replaced by an expression of a man ready to cross his Rubicon.

"Eleanor, I vow, you put me at sixes and sevens, but I shall make my feelings known to you," he declared, seizing her hands, raising them to his lips and planting a very damp kiss on it. It reminded her of the tribute of a friendly pug.

"Now, Harry..."

The determined light in his eyes gleamed again as he moved closer. She retreated an inch. The door opened just as Harry stepped forward again to embrace her.

"Botheration, what is it?" he asked over her shoulder.

"I beg your pardon, Addison," Prescott said with aplomb as he surveyed them through his quizzing glass, "and yours too, Miss Whiting, but during my dance with your cousin she recollected a handkerchief she had misplaced. I have been commissioned to seek it out. I shan't take but a moment. Go on with whatever you were doing."

Flushing, Eleanor moved away from Harry. Prescott, undaunted, ran his hand over a velveteen chair. "No, it isn't there. Would you mind getting up, Addison?" he asked, for Harry had sunk down onto the Egyptian couch. "I just thought I'd check behind those cushions."

Muttering a veiled oath, Harry rose.

"Is that what you are searching for?" Eleanor asked, pointing to a lace handkerchief on the mantel.

Prescott plucked the white square of cloth up. "Well, it is a handkerchief, and a lady's too, judging by the smell of French perfume. So it must be Maria's. Fancy it being in plain view. I do beg your pardon. Go ahead with your proposal, Addison."

"How do you know I planned to propose?" Harry demanded.

Prescott laughed. "I am not a gudgeon. What else could you be doing with the two of you locked in that soulful embrace, except making Miss Whiting an offer of marriage or of carte blanche.''

"Prescott!" Harry was outraged.

"But I know your high sense of propriety," Prescott went on. "And I couldn't miss the way Miss Whiting's eyes shine like stars when she looks at you."

Much to Eleanor's chagrin, both gentlemen now turned their attention to her, Harry seemingly fixed on her eyes.

"If you two gentlemen have finished making me the object of your sport, I should like to leave," Eleanor said icily.

"But Eleanor, we haven't finished," Harry protested.

Prescott shook his head. "Do you mean to say you haven't given him a decision, Miss Whiting?" he asked, clucking his tongue. "The man made you an offer. You must not keep him dangling. But then, that is your habit, is it not?" he murmured so low that only Eleanor could hear the last of his words.

"You'd best speak to Sir Donald first, Addison. Devilish high in the instep he is about matters of propriety, particularly those that concern his daughter.''

"I have been trying to see him," Harry expostulated. "Thought I saw him at White's this afternoon, but I couldn't get him to talk to me."

"Don't let him bully you when you ask for Miss Whiting's hand. Having gone through that interview once I should advise you to be pluck to the old backbone."

"Er, well, thanks for the advice, Prescott."

Prescott waved a languid hand. "Not at all. I shan't begrudge any man the chance to learn from my mistakes," he said, smiling coldly at Eleanor.

CHAPTER SIX

MISTAKE INDEED, Eleanor fumed as she left the ante-room in search of her mother. Faced with the thundercloud expression on her daughter's countenance, Lady Constance suggested an early end to their evening for it was plain as two pins that Harry had botched his proposal to Eleanor.

It was but half an hour later that Lord Prescott made his own departure from King Street. After all that female society he felt in need of male companionship so he pressed on to Watier's where good fellowship could always be found at the green baize tables.

Dame Fortune was with him for once, and his lucky streak lasted until three in the morning. Chief among his victims were Lords Foxworth and Clivebon.

Clivebon paid him off with a laugh and a demand that when they next met he be a trifle less lucky. On the other hand, Foxworth, hemmed and hawwed so much that Prescott took pity on him.

"I can give you time to raise the funds," he said, inhaling a pinch of snuff and offering the mixture to the other man.

Foxworth flushed. "Obliged to you, Prescott, but all I need is a week. Young Whiting's wife owes me a comparable sum. Once she makes good her debt, I shall pay you."

Prescott shut his Sèvres snuff box. "Do you mean Andrew Whiting's wife?" he asked softly.

"Aye, that's the one. Sat down with me at whist this evening and lost near to a thousand pounds."

"Which is a little less than you have lost to me," Prescott pointed out. "Your debt is twelve hundred pounds." He paused for a moment then said smoothly. "But I'll take Mrs. Whiting's note instead and we'll call it even. What say you?"

Foxworth looked baffled. "What do you want with her note?" he asked.

"If the arrangement doesn't please you . . ." Prescott shrugged.

"Didn't say that!" Foxworth uttered a strangled oath and dug into the pocket of his waistcoat. He laid Julia Whiting's note on the table. "We're even then?"

Prescott nodded as he stretched out a languid hand to examine the note. Did Andrew know his young wife had fallen into the briars? Still musing on the matter, he left the card room and stepped out into the night air. He thought of calling up a hack but the brisk walk to Berkeley Square would clear him of the thoughts that had vexed him of late.

He was nearing the door to his residence when he saw a hack stop at the corner. From it emerged young Edward Cassidy and a familiar-looking Cyprian by the name of Fanny.

"Pon rep, Prescott, is that you?" Edward asked, nearly colliding with him at the door.

"Indeed, it is," Prescott replied. "You've had a late night."

"I'm in love, Prescott. In love with Fanny here..." He bussed the woman resoundingly on her cherry-red lips.

"I was under the impression that it was a different female you were in love with," Prescott drawled.

Edward gave a ghastly grin. "You mean Maria Whiting? Dangling after her yourself, aren't you?" He lurched for a moment on the top step of Prescott's residence. "That fortune of hers lures even you. But you don't need it." His voice whined. "I do. But when it comes to a body to warm my bed I'd as lief have Fanny!" He gave Fanny another boisterous kiss.

Prescott turned away, but Edward had caught the look of distaste on the other man's face.

"Don't play the noble one with me, Prescott. Everyone knows about you and Aimée Martine. Courting Miss Eleanor Whiting and keeping Aimée on the side. You'd have kept her while you were married to that Long Meg."

"I would advise you not to say another word, Cassidy," Prescott said coldly.

"Sent your ring back in that bit of muslin, didn't she?" Edward guffawed. "I've heard the stories. She's practically an ape leader now."

It was the last thing he was destined to utter that evening for Prescott dealt him a quick facer, then left him in the street to be tended by a swooning Fanny.

THE NEXT MORNING Eleanor awoke feeling uncommonly listless and dull. She had tossed and turned most of the night, unable to get a wink of sleep until early morning. Whenever her eyes had closed, Prescott's mocking face swam into view. *Odious man— pretending to give Harry advice on winning her.* She would have cheerfully strangled him if Harry hadn't been smiling so idiotishly nearby.

Harry! Too late she remembered her promise to give him a decision some time soon on his offer of marriage. And what answer would that be? If indeed Harry intended to speak to her father today she would need to warn Papa.

"An offer from Harry Addison, eh?" Sir Donald rumbled in the breakfast room as he reached for a plate of ham and darted an appraising eye at his daughter next to him. "Can't say I'm surprised. Fellow's been dangling after you forever."

"Hardly that, Papa," Eleanor replied. "Just this season."

"Seemed like forever," he grunted. "Well? What do you want me to tell him?"

Eleanor speared a piece of pineapple. "Why, Papa, it is not for me to presume to dictate to you...."

Her father snorted. "Don't be missish. You can't hoodwink me for a second. You want me to tell Harry something. What is it? Shall I run him off? Or welcome him into the family?"

The idea of Harry in the family in a permanent way nearly overset Eleanor who choked on the pineapple. "I don't know what you should do."

"Eh what?" Sir Donald nearly stabbed his thumb with his fork. "You don't know. What is this? You've always known before if a gentleman would do or not. Why so missish now?"

"I wish I knew, Papa," Eleanor said in a voice that to her father sounded strangely forlorn. He wished Lady Constance were present and not taking a breakfast tray in her room.

"Do you love him?" he asked abruptly.

"Who? Harry?"

"Who else are we speaking of?" Sir Donald asked, nettled by these shifts in his very own daughter. "He's an agreeable enough person with a goodly income. And you'll have handsome children, I'll say that for him. And he's not a rake, if that's what worries you." He cast a quizzical look her way.

"It does not," she replied with equanimity.

"Three years ago it worried you a good deal," he reminded her.

A ghost of a smile touched her lips. "Three years ago Harry wasn't proposing."

"No, Prescott was," her father said. "Do you wish it were he proposing now instead of Harry?"

"Really, Papa, the things you ask of me," Eleanor expostulated. "I come in this morning to have a civil word with you about Harry and what must you do but bring up Prescott, whom you claim to loath."

"Oh, I don't loath him," Sir Donald protested. "Not even a mild dislike, though I admit I was angry at the way you two made a public spectacle of yourselves."

"Public spectacle, Papa? I've never heard you say such a thing before."

"Not a thing I relish saying to you," he said gruffly. "But sending him his ring back in that muslin wasn't the thing for a lady to do."

"Would you have rather I boxed his ears?"

"That I might," he conceded, "but don't let's quarrel about him. His offer isn't before us, or is it?" No sooner had the query left his lips than his daughter immediately bristled.

"Of course it isn't," she said.

"Then it's Harry that concerns us." Sire Donald looked wistfully at his plate. "What will it be?" he asked impatiently. "I'll wish him to Jericho if you say so or welcome him with open arms. You can't keep him dangling forever. You'll get a reputation as a flirt."

Eleanor bit her lip. "Could you just tell Harry if he does offer that you need a little more time to consider the matter?"

Sir Donald gulped a mouthful of egg. "*I* need the time?"

"Please, Papa," she said.

Sir Donald sighed. He could never refuse Eleanor anything when she turned that face to him.

"Very well. But you will inform me when *I* have reached a decision, won't you?" he said grumpily and returned to his breakfast.

EDWARD CASSIDY STARED into his pier glass, wincing at the black-and-blue bruise about his eye.

"You're lucky," said the physician. "You might have broken your nose. What happened?"

"Footpads," Edward muttered, not about to reveal the true happenstance to anyone. How dared Prescott strike him? He would revenge this insult if it were the last thing he did.

"Ow," he exclaimed, pulling away from the doctor's probing fingers. "Off with you, you quack!"

The doctor snapped shut his bag and left.

"Ooh, ducks, I think you got him angry," Fanny cooed from the other side of the room where she was admiring her nails.

"What are you doing here?" he demanded.

"Here, now. You hired me for the night, didn't you? And you haven't paid me yet."

Edward threw back his head and roared, "Get out! The night's over. Away with you!"

"I've got friends, I have."

"I'm sure I know precisely the type of friend you have, my little beauty."

"Well I'm sure there will be many who will laugh when they hear you were dealt a facer by that Lord Prescott. And who was it who drove you here, I might ask— Ow!" she exclaimed as Edward pinched one of her ears.

"If I ever hear you say a word about what happened tonight, a word—" he pulled her ear lobe again. "—I'll throttle you, I swear it, Fanny."

"I won't—I promise," she said, taken back by the change in him. Quickly, she grabbed her wrap and scurried out of his room. It wasn't until later that she realized that he still hadn't given her a groat for her night's work.

MR. ROBERT ALDRIDGE, man of business to Mrs. Edgewater, looked up quickly at the gentleman striding into his office. One look was sufficient to bring him to his feet. "Lord Prescott!" he exclaimed.

"Hallo, Aldridge," Prescott said, smiling.

The two had been long acquainted for Aldridge had been the previous Lord Prescott's man of business and indeed served in that capacity for many of the ton.

"Pray, what can I do for you, my lord?"

"It's about Oakmore. I believe I may have a buyer for the property. Mr. Andrew Whiting has expressed interest in seeing it. I have already talked to my aunt and she said to direct all enquiries to you. I believe Andrew will wish to see the estate some time soon."

Mr. Aldridge frowned. "I am obliged to post to Northumbria immediately. You've caught me just as I was leaving some last-minute instruction for my clerk. One of my clients, Lord Fenley, asked me to come for a visit. You know him, don't you?"

"Indeed, I do," Prescott said. Fenley was one of his father's oldest cronies. "He is laid up with gout, I hear."

"And dyspepsia, but he has as much life left to him as any other man. He is always so interested in the news of town. Particularly news about his heir, Edward Cassidy. He is his great-nephew and Fenley dotes on him."

"Well, if you are promised to Fenley I can ask Andrew to wait. Or he can journey to Oakmore and see for himself. The servants are still there and can put him up for the night."

"Yes, of course, he could do that," Aldridge agreed. "I shall just write him a letter and then he is free to inspect the estate himself. He'll find it very neglected."

"He's been forewarned," Prescott replied. After Aldridge had blotted the letter with sand and handed it to him he said, "I shall give this to him. And do give Lord Fenley my best."

Thinking of Lord Fenley brought Edward and their mill the night before back to Prescott's mind. He sighed, not in the least proud of his conduct. Brawling in the streets, even if the streets were deserted, was not the way a gentleman conducted himself.

And yet he did not regret striking Edward. His words were unconscionable! How dared he throw Aimée up in his face, hinting that Prescott's alliance with her was no different from Edward's with Fanny. Pre-

posterous pup—to accuse him of intending to keep
Aimée while married to Eleanor! And how dared he
insult Eleanor like that! Ape-leader, indeed!

Frowning, Prescott descended the stairs of Aldridge's building. Three years ago Eleanor had been
charming and beautiful and witty. He had known at
first sight that he wanted her for a wife. He had fully
intended to give up Aimée, but he did not like having
Eleanor order him to do so as a condition of their
marriage. It had struck him as lacking a certain trust.

He picked up the reins to his phaeton. For the first
time since he had received his ring back from Eleanor
he was obliged to consider the situation from her point
of view. Had he seemed no better than Edward with
Fanny the previous night? Had he flaunted Aimée before the ton? Prescott searched his conscience and
didn't fully like what he saw there.

AIMÉE GAZED AT THE CANVAS and wrinkled up her
nose. "I know it is just the first sitting I have done for
you, *Monsieur*, but I cannot say that I am too pleased
by what you have painted."

John Sebastian gave a rueful laugh. "Oh, Mademoiselle Martine, I know. And I will improve. It's just
that my mind is distracted."

"Indeed?" Aimée asked, drawing the dressing gown
tighter about her. Sebastian was a tall, gawky painter,
nothing at all like Armand, but she had enough feeling for art to know that he had talent. Of course, she
would not want her face used if he didn't improve the
painting.

"In my contact with artists I have discovered that it
is inevitably women or drink that cause such distraction of the mind. Which is it?" she asked kindly.

"Women."

"Ah, yes," Aimée said, comfortable with this topic as she watched him rinse his paintbrushes. "Women and men, an age-old problem."

"Her name is Isabelle Rush, and she was my model, a lovely young thing. Innocent. Here is my painting of her." From a stack of canvases he pulled one out.

Aimée gazed into a dewy face and felt for a moment a pang of jealousy.

"We were in love and determined to marry, only she fell in love with a gentleman."

Aimée felt a moment's sympathy for the young model. Falling in love with a gentleman was not the way to happiness for women like them.

"And he broke her heart?"

"Of course. She fled to the country. I didn't care. I would love her and marry her anyway. But she wants no part of me."

"Sometimes after having one's heart broken, a woman needs time to recover. I know whereof I speak. But someday your Isabelle will forget her gentleman and be happy with someone else. Someone who is quite different from her gentleman, someone like you."

He looked at her curiously, the expression in her eyes rather wise and . . .

"One moment, Aimée...please...if you would sit down again. I must paint you as I see you now...hold that look...."

With a sigh, Aimée returned to her chair. Her back was near to breaking, but in the interest of Art she would endure another half hour of penance. Besides, it was nice to be destined for immortality.

CHAPTER SEVEN

JULIA WHITING FINGERED the keys of the pianoforte, picking out a plaintive melody. Always before she had found comfort in music, but today the music sheets in front of her might as well have been Greek.

"Julia, my dear?"

Her fingers crashed down on the keyboard as Andrew stuck his head into the music room. In her cream-coloured muslin she cut a delightful picture of domesticity, her appearance giving no clue to her heart's turmoil.

"Still practicing your beloved Beethoven?" he teased.

"I mean to do so until I get it right," she said, striking a wrong chord yet again.

"It's most unlike you to worry about your music," Andrew said, pecking her on the cheek. "Confess, do you not feel quite the thing?"

"Why of course, Andrew," she said, attempting that tricky part of the sonata once again. Did he suspect? For a moment panic seized her. Maybe it would be better if she confessed everything. But what if he thrust her aside? She would not be able to endure his rejection.

"I am not in your black books am I, my dear?" he enquired.

"Oh, Andrew, don't be absurd!" she exclaimed. "As though I could hold anything against you!"

"You are an angel. I can't get over how lucky I was to find you. When I think of all the females Papa wanted me to marry..." He chuckled. "Lady Alice Tremaine has become excessively clutch-fisted now, and as for Eliza Lovell she has taken to gambling and her husband is nearly reduced to penury."

"Poor creature. Just imagine how she must feel."

"I think the husband has got the worst of that match," Andrew said, oblivious to the anxiety in his wife's eyes. "When he married her he didn't know she had this propensity for gambling. Why, she married him under false pretenses." He gave her a hug. "I am off to my lesson with Jackson. We have the rout party tonight at Sir Thomas Bolling's. I suppose you will look as beautiful as always!" He gave her a cheerful wave goodbye.

Julia collapsed on a nearby sofa. False pretenses indeed. The words applied to herself as much as they did to poor Eliza Lovell. And she had only herself to blame. How could she pay off the odious moneylenders? And even more pressing was her debt to Lord Foxworth which was due on Friday.

With her mind so distracted she left the music room and went back up to her bedchamber. She tried to divert herself by thinking about what she would wear to Sir Thomas's rout party. She had that azure silk, cut in the Grecian fashion and she would wear it with her turquoise necklace.

A pretty frown creased her brow at the thought of the jewellery. Andrew had given her a sapphire necklace during their courtship, and he bestowed a diamond bracelet upon her for their wedding.

"But I can't sell these," she said, speaking the thought that had been lurking in her mind as soon as her fingers touched the jewels. They were Andrew's special gifts to her.

Her hands delved further into the jewel box. Other pieces had been given to her by her mother-in-law, who had stigmatized them as fusty and heavy.

Surely if she sold these pieces no one would miss them. With a giddy sense of relief Julia bent her blonde head over the box. A topaz pin. An emerald brooch. A very ugly ruby necklace. Now she knew how she would pay off her debts.

When a knock sounded on her bedchamber door, she dropped the topaz pin on the floor.

"Yes?"

"Lord Prescott has called, ma'am," said her maid.

She picked up the pin and returned the jewels to their case. She chanced a quick look at herself in the pier glass and then descended the Adam stairs to find Prescott in the blue drawing room admiring a Ming vase.

"Ah, Mrs. Whiting, I do hope I have not called you from pressing matters," Prescott said. Was it his imagination or did Andrew's wife look rather more pale than was fashionable?

"Not at all, my lord," Julia said with equanimity. "Pray, won't you be seated. I'm sorry that Andrew is not home to receive you."

He seated himself on the Egyptian couch while she took the Trafalgar chair opposite. "Your butler told me that he only left a few minutes ago. Would you give him this?" He pulled Aldridge's letter out from his pocket and explained what it was.

"Thank you, my lord," she said, taking the letter.
"I'm sure that Andrew will be grateful for your help
in this matter."

Now that his mission was accomplished Prescott
should have been taking his leave. Instead, his dark
eyes held a mesmerizing glint as he gazed her way.
Remembering his reputation as a rake, Julia felt a
frisson of alarm.

"Would you like some sherry, my lord?" she asked
to cover her nervousness.

"No, thank you," Prescott said. How the devil
could he delicately broach the topic of her debt to
Foxworth? Far better to take his fences in a rush.
"Mrs. Whiting, last evening you lost a thousand
pounds to Lord Foxworth, did you not?"

The colour drained from Julia's face.

"Foxworth and I sat down together at Watier's later
last night. He had the misfortune to lose to me and as
payment he included the bond that you owe him."

"Well then, I owe you a thousand pounds, my lord.
Are you here to dun me?"

"No, not in the least," he said quickly. "I came
here, well, to reassure you about the debt. If you don't
have the money perhaps we can make a suitable arrangement."

These words were gently spoken, but they fell on
Julia's ears like a clap of thunder. She was a married
female without funds of her own. What suitable arrangements could Prescott be hinting at? Her heart
sank.

She would have to pay him the thousand pounds or
be obliged to accommodate him in bed. She shuddered at the thought.

"Mrs. Whiting? Did you hear me?" Prescott asked, rather perplexed by her stricken countenance.

"Indeed I did," she said coldly. "And you may rest assured you will have your thousand pounds by Friday. Now, if you will excuse me, I find I have some errands to run," she said, thus cutting short what had been for her a most disagreeable call.

THE STOUT GENTLEMAN hastily entering the reading room of White's and burying himself in a copy of the *Racing News* attracted a modicum of interest from the habitués of the club.

"Are the Runners after you, Donald?" enquired Lord Jaynes, putting down his copy of the *Gentleman's Monthly*.

Sir Donald snorted. "If it were only the Runners. You're lucky you never married, Jaynes."

"Of that I am fully aware," Lord Jaynes replied, from the comfortable vantage point of an unmarried man. "Are you in fear of your wife, then? Has she sent the footman after you to drag you home?"

"No, no. It ain't Constance," Sir Donald said, a little peeved by his friend's good-natured jesting. "It's Eleanor, my daughter. The shifts I've been put to."

"Trying to marry her off?" Jaynes cocked his head toward his friend.

Sir Donald snorted. "Eleanor ain't the type of chit to be married off unless she wants it. That's the trouble, she doesn't know whether she wants him or not."

"Handsome Harry Addison?" Lord Jaynes enquired with a pinch of snuff between thumb and forefinger. "I've heard nothing against him."

Sir Donald gave his friend a measuring look. "Nor anything for him, I daresay? Rather like a taste of bread pudding. It won't make you smack your lips in anticipation, nor will it give you a stomach ache later."

"What does bread pudding have to do with anything?" Lord Jaynes asked petulantly. "Thought we were talking about Addison."

But all of Sir Donald's shifts, were for nought. No sooner had he stepped out of the reading room, intending to make a quick dash for the door and his curricle, than Harry Addison pounced on him.

"On your way home, Sir Donald?" Harry asked, swinging his malacca cane.

"No." Sir Donald coloured under Addison's innocent gaze. "I mean I was on my way to Manton's, but I'll spare you a moment. We can talk on the way." He couldn't very well avoid the man forever.

Harry obligingly fell in with Sir Donald, as they walked out of the club. "Sir Donald, surely by this time you must know that I should like to marry Eleanor."

"You would, would you," Sir Donald said gloomily.

"Well, yes!" Harry said, somewhat surprised by this reaction. "She's the dearest, sweetest female of my acquaintance."

Sir Donald tried in vain to reconcile this image of a dear sweet female with the headstrong creature who resided under his roof. "Just how many females are you acquainted with?"

"Sir Donald, I assure you! I have never made a habit of the petticoat line. My words were meant as praise for your daughter, not as a confession."

Sir Donald shook his head. It was vain to hope that Addison was anything other than a very dull dog. Eleanor would be bored to tears within a month of their marriage. "It's not that I have anything against you, Addison," he said to the other man, as they dodged an irate coachman, "but one shouldn't rush into marriage."

"Rush? But I've known her these past three months. That's not rushing, sir."

"No," Sir Donald agreed. "But just the same..."

A carriage cutting its corners rather too sharply for safety brought an end to the baronet's words.

"Watch where you are going!" he shouted to the driver. Never had he seen such ham-handed driving. The streets of London were daily filling with more obstacles.

"Sir, I have heard from several sources that when Prescott offered for your daughter, it was after an acquaintanceship of only one month. And she accepted him."

"Aye," Sir Donald said, seizing on this straw. "But she has learned from that experience, which is why I'd advise you to go slowly, Addison."

"But she's had three years to get over him. Are you saying she still nurses a tendre for him?"

"No, I think she thoroughly dislikes him," Sir Donald said confidently.

"Then there is no obstacle in our path."

"Obstacle?" Sir Donald looked absently around him. "None whatsoever that I can see, Addison."

A broad grin spread on Harry's cheeks. "Thank you, Sir Donald," he said. "I knew that you would not oppose my offer for Eleanor."

"Yes. No. That is—" Now how in thunderation had that happened, Sir Donald wondered to himself as Harry hurried off. And how in the world would he ever explain it to Eleanor?

AT THE VERY MOMENT Sir Donald was giving Harry a clear path to her door, Eleanor was riding in the Park with her sister-in-law. She had always enjoyed riding, thinking it a superior sport to being cooped up in a carriage and had prevailed upon Julia to accompany her. But Julia did not seem to be enjoying the blue skies and mild wind. The thought of Julia's debts passed fleetingly through Eleanor's mind, but the day was too fine for such an uncomfortable subject so Eleanor prudently did not broach it.

The two ladies encountered many of their acquaintance enjoying the air. Mrs. Drummond Burrell rode past, as did Maria accompanied by two of her suitors, and Diana and her husband, Philip Hawthorne. They stopped for a moment's conversation which had to do with Lady Fogarty's musicale, in which Julia had consented to play the pianoforte and Diana the harp.

"And what will you play, Eleanor?" Diana asked.

"Heavens, I won't. You both know that I play abominably. I deem it my contribution to attend and applaud wildly when you have performed."

"Have I told you that I am to have my portrait painted?" Diana asked. "There is a new painter, Sebastian by name. Isn't it exciting? You should think about having yours done!" Diana said with a gay wave as she and her husband drove off.

"My portrait painted. I don't think I would have such a thing done, but what of you, Julia? Do you think Andrew would like it?"

The mere mention of Andrew caused Julia to burst into tears.

"Good heavens," Eleanor exclaimed, bewildered by this transformation of her sister-in-law into a watering pot. "My dear, if you don't like the idea of sitting for a painting, and very painful it can be to sit for hours at a time, you need only say so."

"It's not the painting," Julia said, pulling a lace handkerchief out of her reticule. "It's Andrew."

"Oh. Does Andrew want his portrait painted? Odd that he never voiced such a wish to me."

"That's not it," Julia said thickly.

Eleanor waited. She knew Julia was not a keen horsewoman and she was reprimanding herself for having tendered the invitation to ride.

"What's amiss, Julia?" she asked kindly.

Mrs. Whiting attempted to speak but could only dissolve again into her handkerchief.

"Is it about your debts?" Eleanor asked delicately.

Julia nodded. She wiped her eyes and blew her nose.

"Yes. And I must come up with a thousand pounds by Friday or else the worst penalty imaginable will be extracted from me."

"I know that the moneylenders charge exorbitant interest," Eleanor said, quick sympathy showing in her blue eyes.

"It's not the moneylenders I'm afraid of. It's Prescott."

"Prescott?" Eleanor was astonished. "How is he involved in this coil?"

"I own him a thousand pounds," Julia said. "And he threatens to make the most odious advances to me if I don't pay it."

CHAPTER EIGHT

PRESCOTT MAKING ADVANCES toward her sister-in law? Was Julia queer in the attic? Never would she have believed such a thing, but Julia was not the sort of female to make up stories.

"He is the most odious man imaginable," Julia went on. "I fully understand why you didn't wish to marry him three years ago."

"My dear, I know that Prescott is abominable, but I wouldn't have thought him sunk so low as to throw a lure at you."

"You forget that I am a married lady," Julia said. "I know when a gentleman is a gentleman and when he is not."

"Then you should have boxed Prescott's ears or told Andrew. He would not stand for anyone insulting his wife." Her voice trailed off as she met Julia's eyes, and the two of them contemplated the inevitable.

"He'd challenge Prescott on the spot," Julia said hollowly, "and we both know that Andrew is not the crack shot Prescott is. The only thing which will serve is for me to pay him and in the meantime treat him with perfect indifference." But that would be, she was obliged to admit to herself, rather difficult since she did not know where she would get the money.

Eleanor was considerably shaken by Julia's news and continued to dwell on this new side of Prescott's character when she reached home. He had been a notorious rake in his salad days, not above setting up one high flyer after another. And yet, she had not thought that his taste ran toward newly married females, particularly one as sweet-natured as Julia.

Why was Prescott toying with Julia? Was it because Julia was Eleanor's sister by marriage? Was Prescott still angered by what had happened three years ago? Was the ruin of Andrew's marriage his ultimate revenge?

THE PROBLEM with dangling after a chit like Maria Whiting, Prescott thought to himself as he put his team of high-steppers through their paces round the Park was that any man of sense became rapidly bored with what passed for conversation in her company. Five topics had he introduced and on each she had agreed eagerly with whatever opinion he had offered. She was sweet and pretty enough, but he might sustain a fever of the brain if he persisted in trying to engage her in any type of colloquy.

It wasn't really conversation, of course, that Prescott wanted from Maria, but information. He was disinclined to poke his nose into others' business. Yet his conscience would not allow him to stand by and see Edward take advantage of an innocent chit like Maria. He looked quickly at his companion. She did indeed resemble an angel with those porcelain cheeks and that glazed smile.

"Are you planning to attend Lady Fremont's rout party this evening?" he enquired.

"Oh, yes," Maria replied breathlessly. "Aunt Lavinia says that it will be such a squeeze."

"You will allow me one of your dances, I hope?" he drawled.

"Yes. But not the first." A stricken look came into her eyes, then was chased away by a far different expression as she explained that she had promised Mr. Edward Cassidy the first dance.

"Cassidy is your devoted suitor." Prescott drew his Welshbreds to the side to allow another carriage to pass.

Maria's eyes shone. "Well, he is so attentive and charming. He is Aunt Lavinia's favorite." As a frown knit Prescott's craggy brow Maria realized that she might have committed a solecism in praising one suitor while in the company of another. And yet she did not believe that Prescott was truly pursuing her.

Her aunt might think so, but Maria, young though she was, knew when a gentleman was interested in her. So she did not scruple to confide to him now all she felt about her wonderful Edward. And Prescott, she discovered, was a good listener.

But Maria would have felt quite betrayed had she been able to read his thoughts, thoughts that became even grimmer when he brought Maria home and met Lady Vyne.

"Oh, Maria. And Lord Prescott, do come in and have some tea," Lady Vyne entreated. "Mr. Cassidy has called."

"Why, Mr. Cassidy, what happened to your eye?" Maria asked in astonishment, rushing to greet him.

"He has just been telling me all about it!" Lady Vyne declared as Prescott took the chair his hostess indicated. "Footpads set upon him last evening. He was thoroughly outnumbered. Three to one, wasn't it, Mr. Cassidy?''

"Quite so," Edward said uncomfortably as Prescott eyed him through his quizzing glass.

"But he managed to fight them all off," Lady Vyne reported with great satisfaction. "I vow, I would give a monkey to see those ruffians.''

Prescott accepted the cup of tea his hostess offered. "But why would you wish to be set upon by the trio that damaged Edward?''

"Oh, I don't wish to be set upon," Lady Vyne said with a shudder. Her courage fell short of this mark. "I merely wished to see for myself the damage inflicted by Edward. A broken nose, you did say?''

"Er, yes," Edward drawled, as Prescott rubbed his nose. "But really, I don't believe such matters are intended for a young lady like Maria."

"Oh, I don't mind," Maria said immediately. "Indeed, I'd love to hear more about your heroism."

"It was nothing," Cassidy said, running a finger between his collar points. "Pray, consider the matter closed.''

This modesty put him even higher in both ladies' estimation.

Prescott accurately assessed that any word against Edward to Lady Vyne or Maria would fall on deaf ears. Although he had overstayed his visit to Maria, he was not about to leave and allow Edward to press his attentions on her. His reluctance to depart was eagerly interpreted by Lady Vyne as proof of Lord Prescott's own interest in her young charge.

"Depend upon it," she said later after both gentlemen had left, "you have scored a notable hit. To have attached Prescott. Good heavens, child, the caps that have been set at him! Not even your own cousin, Eleanor, was able to land him. What did you talk about on your drive in the Park?''

Maria reflected a moment. ''Actually, Aunt, he asked a good many questions about Edward's fixing an interest in me.''

''Really?'' A superb smile lifted Lady Vyne's lips. ''Prescott is indeed dangling after you! Conversation about Edward, indeed. He wants to know whether Edward has stolen a march on him. What did you tell him?''

''That I quite liked Edward, of course,'' Maria said naively. ''And I must own, Aunt, that I find Edward more handsome than Prescott.''

''You mustn't make up your mind too fast,'' Lady Vyne clucked. ''Prescott is very deep in the pocket, not that Edward is a pauper. He has his estates in Cornwall, and will inherit a goodly sum of money when his uncle, Lord Fenley, dies.''

Mention of Edward's fortune put Maria in mind of her own rumoured fortune.

''I do not like pretending that I have a vast fortune, Aunt Lavinia. I hate shams.''

''It is not a sham, merely misinformation that has been set about, and which we will set to rights soon enough. Now let us consider what you are to wear to Lady Fremont's party tonight.''

''When will we set the matter of my fortune to rights, Aunt?'' Maria asked, in her bedchamber, examining the gowns that Lady Lavinia drew out for her perusal.

''After you are married,'' Lady Vyne murmured. ''What think you of this colour?''

"Aunt, you are not serious! I cannot wait to inform Edward about my lack of fortune until after we exchange vows! Why, that would be ... dishonest!"

"Now, Maria, I have had more experience in these matters than you. And while you say having people believe you possess a large fortune is dishonest, it is not. It is merely letting them believe what they wish to believe for the time being. I can count on one hand the number of females who have been brilliantly matched without a fortune. Most gentlemen do look for well-dowried wives. But not all. Your sweetness and beauty will carry the day without your fortune. Trust me."

"Then why must I pretend to be an heiress? Why, I doubt very much if Father will be able to raise my portion."

"I have my reasons," Lady Vyne said. "I have not failed you yet, have I?"

"No, Aunt. And I am grateful."

Lady Vyne gathered her niece into a scented embrace. "Don't fall into a pelter about your fortune. I'd wager a monkey that neither of your chief admirers, Mr. Cassidy nor Lord Prescott cares a fig about it."

IN THIS RESPECT Lady Vyne was wrong, for one of those two gentlemen was indeed very interested in Maria's nonexistent fortune. Mr. Edward Cassidy's habits of gaming and high living had necessitated certain uncomfortable economies, and when pressed by his creditors he had been forced to turn to the money-lenders.

Of course when his uncle Fenley died all would be well. But the fellow did seem to enjoy more robust good health than anyone with sixty years in his dish had any right to.

After leaving the Vyne residence Edward drove to the City. He had heard of a certain person, Grimes, who would buy rings and watches, and he was searching for the address of the broker when he nearly collided with Julia Whiting.

"Oh, I do beg your pardon!" he exclaimed as Julia almost bounced off his chest. "Why, it's Mrs. Whiting, isn't it?"

"Er, yes, Mr. Cassidy. Pray, forgive me for walking right into you, I fear I was trying to find an address and wasn't watching where I was going."

"Perhaps I can be of assistance."

"No, I don't think so," Julia said, twirling her parasol.

He smiled winningly at her. "Mrs. Whiting, I feel obliged to point out that I am probably better acquainted with this section of town than you. Ladies do not walk about here unescorted. You will save yourself considerable distress if you allow me to escort you."

"But I don't know where I am going. I mean...oh, heavens, I sound so idiotish," Julia said. "I am looking for a Mr. Grimes."

"Grimes!" Edward exclaimed. "What do you have to do with Mr. Grimes."

Julia flushed. "It's a private matter."

"Of course. Well, I can direct you to Grimes's address. Do you intend to conduct your business with him personally?"

"Why, yes. Why not?"

Edward shrugged. "It's just that a female in need of funds might not be able to extract as advantageous a bargain from him. A gentleman acting in your behalf might be of greater assistance."

"But I have no one...."

"You have me, if you wish," Edward said with a bow. "I am at your disposal. I think I will get a fair price for whatever it is you wish to sell to him."

Julia hesitated a moment, but Edward looked so charming and helpful. Moreover he was dangling after Maria, practically family as Lady Vyne was wont to say.

"Very well. I must admit the idea of actually confronting Mr. Grimes and arguing with him about the price of what I wish to sell was most disquieting."

"What do you have to sell?" Edward asked.

As an answer Julia thrust a handkerchief containing the ruby pin and an emerald bracelet toward him. Edward inhaled a quick breath. These were heirlooms or he was the king of China. And how much did Mrs. Whiting wish to receive for them? Reverently, he took the jewels from her, as he put the question.

"I need at least a thousand pounds," Julia said. With the thousand pounds she could take care of Prescott.

"A thousand?" Edward stroked his chin. She'd get twice that if he was the bargainer he thought he was. "I'll try, Mrs. Whiting. Now, have you brought a carriage?"

"My maid is waiting back there." Julia indicated a vehicle farther down the street.

"Good. You get inside it and wait. I'll see Grimes and bring you the thousand pounds."

"Oh, thank you, Mr. Cassidy. I feel as though a burden has been lifted from my shoulders!"

"So do I," Edward said chuckling to himself as he disappeared up the stairs. He descended twenty minutes later and strolled down to Julia's carriage.

"This is your thousand pounds, I believe," he said, presenting her with a roll of bills.

"Oh, Mr. Cassidy, you did it! I should have been lost without your help."

"No thanks necessary," Edward said. He bowed and left, a broad smile on his face. His own financial troubles had disappeared thanks to that feather-brained chit. Grimes was as shrewd as they come, but he had seen the jewels as being worth nearly five thousand pounds and had agreed quickly to give two thousand for them. Julia had taken half, which still left a thousand for Edward himself.

It had been, he thought with another chuckle, a very good day.

CHAPTER NINE

EDWARD'S GOOD FEELINGS continued into the evening's rout party at Lady Fremont's. He acquitted himself well in the ballroom and played the role of devoted suitor to Maria Whiting. With his pockets temporarily filled, he coaxed Maria into her second waltz with him, and she had to be discouraged from standing up with him a third time.

"The proprieties must be observed," Lady Vyne said, dispatching Eleanor across the crowded ballroom to separate the young couple. Edward certainly seemed to be sitting in Maria's pocket, Eleanor thought. She mentioned this observation to Julia and soon discovered that her sister-in-law had become young Edward's champion, full of praise for his civility and manners. And Julia's opinion must count for something—as must her disapproval, Eleanor considered, when she saw Prescott striding past.

She was still puzzling over his lordship's attempt to seduce Julia. True, he had dabbled in the petticoat line before, but he was not a blackguard. Would Julia continue to turn him a cold shoulder? Few women were immune when he turned his full attention to them, as she herself could attest. Remembering, she felt the colour rise in her cheeks until they were nearly the shade of her peach-coloured silk. She was glad to be diverted by the task set by her aunt.

"Then you must dance with me, Miss Whiting," Edward declared, and she laughingly allowed him to lead her out. "I am eager to know you better, since you are Maria's cousin."

"My sister-in-law Julia speaks highly of you," she said, falling into the rhythm of the quadrille. Edward was an excellent dancer.

A faint smile curved his lips. How provident had been his encounter with Julia. "I'm most obliged to Mrs. Whiting. But on the other hand there are those who would speak ill of me."

"Such as?" Her hazel eyes held a challenge.

"Lord Prescott, for one," he answered promptly.

"Why should he?"

"It is a complete puzzle to me," Edward said, dancing her expertly away from the crush of couples clogging one end of the room. "Hitherto I have always counted him a friend and indeed have entertained him at home on occasion."

"What could have caused a breach between you?" Eleanor asked, genuinely curious.

"The only thing I can think of is Maria. I suppose he is so accustomed to enthralling females that it may not set well with him that Maria likes me." He sighed. "It wouldn't surprise me if Prescott started the vilest rumours possible about me and my character."

"He's hardly a saint himself."

Edward laughed. "Yes, I know. But he is a determined rival."

Eleanor was silent, pondering this new evidence of the seriousness of Prescott's courtship of Maria. True he had been dangling after Maria since her come-out party, but she hadn't paid much attention. Now, according to Edward, Prescott was determined to win Maria's hand.

"It would help enormously, Miss Whiting, in my courtship of Maria, if I felt that I had your support," Edward said.

She smiled. "Of course, Mr. Cassidy, and I think I can safely say that you have my Aunt Lavinia's support and my sister-in-law, Julia's, as well."

"You are most generous," Edward said gratefully, unable to suppress a happy smile. He bent over and kissed Eleanor's hand when their dance ended, a salute that was not missed by either Prescott or Harry Addison. It was Harry who tasked her on the propriety of allowing young gentlemen to kiss her in public view.

"Would you rather he kissed my hand in private?" Eleanor asked, astonished. "Do be sensible, Harry. Edward was just grateful that I would do him a favour with Maria, that's all. It is she whom he is dangling after, not me."

"Then it is her hand he should be kissing, not yours," Harry said, and she looked at her handsome beau more closely.

"Harry, are you jealous?"

"No. Yes. Dash it all, Eleanor, I have been trying to find a private moment with you all evening. I had a devil of a time running down your father today. He told you about our conversation, I suppose?"

"No," Eleanor said, with a feeling of foreboding.

"He agrees to our match."

"What?" Eleanor exclaimed so loudly that Lady Jersey, a few yards away, turned and stared. So that was the reason her father had bolted into his book room this afternoon and had refused to accompany them to the rout. When she got home she would tell him a thing or two! Unfortunately, at the moment she had her hands full with Harry, who looked bound and determined to declare himself in the ballroom if necessary. Finally she managed to persuade him to step out onto the balcony for a moment.

Harry was delighted to comply. "So with Sir Donald's approval all that is left is your decision."

"My decision," Eleanor murmured. "Oh, Harry, I don't know what to say. I fear that I am one of these dreadful females who makes a muddle out of every offer a gentleman may tender.

"Is there some other offer before you?" he asked quietly. "Edward Cassidy, perhaps?"

"What? Oh, no. Edward is Maria's suitor."

"Then Prescott?"

"Prescott?" Her voice almost failed her. "No, he is Maria's suitor too, not mine. Please, Harry. I will give you a decision, as soon as I can. Now, do you think we might step back inside? The draught is beginning to give me a chill."

"Of course," Harry said, "but first—" He picked up her hand and kissed it. It still reminded her of being nuzzled by a pup.

ACROSS THE BALLROOM Julia Whiting was trying with all her might to keep a civil tongue in her head as her husband spoke to Lord Prescott about his coming trip to Oakmore.

"Do you think to stay a se'ennight would be too much for the estate?" Andrew asked Prescott now.

"Not at all. But I warn you that it is dreadfully neglected. And you must not neglect your own wife," he said gallantly, "for a whole week. There are some who might steal her away."

These light-hearted words brought a smile to Andrew's lips, but Julia went rigid. Was it possible that Prescott intended to use Andrew's absence as a way of pressing his suit? The man was more than a blackguard!

"If anyone does try and steal my Julia, he'll have me to contend with," Andrew said, putting a protecting arm about his wife.

Prescott smiled, bowed and moved away.

"Must you go to Wiltshire, Andrew?" Julia asked, linking her fingers with his.

"Now, my dear, we have been over this before. I need to look at the estate."

"Let me come to Wiltshire with you!"

"Julia!" he expostulated. "You heard Lord Prescott. Oakmore is in no condition to receive you. I must say that I am flattered that you would endure such deprivations for the sake of my company, but really I could not let you." He chucked her under the chin. "I shall be back as soon as I can."

With that promise Julia had to be content, but she was not reassured when she found Prescott's measuring gaze upon her when she glanced his way. Odious, odious man.

She fled into the refreshment room where her pallor attracted the concern of Eleanor.

"Julia, what's amiss?"

"Oh, Eleanor, I am so glad you are here. I vow, I can't think straight."

"That makes two of us," Eleanor confided. "Did I tell you that Harry has offered for me?"

"No, has he?" Julia said, momentarily diverted from her own troubles. "What have you told him?"

"That's the thing. I haven't. Papa approves of the match. But what distresses you? It's not Andrew's trip to Wiltshire that has put you on end? If you don't wish to stay on at Cavendish Square, you may come to us."

Julia seized upon those innocent words with the frenzy of a drowning woman grasping a log.

"Dear Eleanor, would you stay with me at Cavendish Square? I know it is a good deal to ask, but I'm afraid of that man."

"Do you mean Prescott? My word, Julia, what has he done?"

"He is continuing to act in the most unconscionable way toward me, Eleanor. Indeed, I fear that if Andrew leaves London, he may press his suit even more ardently. That's why you must come and stay with me. Say you will, please."

The pleading look in Julia's eyes settled the matter for Eleanor, and she gave her assent to the scheme. The look of relief that flooded her sister-in-law's face made her wonder even more about Prescott and those pernicious advances.

Almost against her will she looked for him in the Fremont ballroom, frowning slightly as she failed to find his tall, elegant person.

"Looking for someone, Miss Whiting?" a voice asked and she jumped to find Lord Prescott at her elbow.

"Oh, Prescott, you startled me," she scolded.

"I beg pardon. No doubt you were looking for Harry."

"Harry?" She was thrown back by this query and by the arrogant smile on his face. "No, I was not seeking Harry."

"Good. Then let me beg for the waltz underway."

"I am promised to someone else. Captain Dunbarton."

"Ah yes... and here he comes," he said, nodding at the Captain who had worked his way through the crowd. "Good evening, Dennis, Miss Whiting has just confided her dilemma to me, one that I'm duty-bound to share with you. She had given you the waltz underway, not remembering that she had already promised it to me earlier. Naturally she is prostrate with remorse and can't think how she came to be so shatterbrained. I daresay you won't mind if she keeps her promise to me and lets you have a later one."

"No... that is..."

"Good of you, Dennis," Prescott said and swept Eleanor off in the waltz.

"Shatterbrained, indeed. I don't suppose it bothers you a whit that the captain will consider me a veritable widgeon from now on."

"No one would dare think you that," Prescott said. He gazed down at her, acutely aware of the eyes that flashed with just a bit of temper and of the sweet curve of her lips. With a heroic effort of will he brought his mind back to the task at hand, namely to advise Eleanor not to allow Edward to win Maria's hand.

She was the only female who would serve this purpose. Lady Lavinia was too idiotish to be sensible, and Maria herself was utterly besotted by Edward. Prescott had thought that Julia Whiting might be of some assistance in this quarter, but she seemed strangely cool and skittish of late. When he merely tried to acknowledge the thousand pounds she had dispatched to his residence earlier today, she had seemed to freeze. So it would have to be Eleanor.

For her part, Eleanor, wished the dance were over and done with. To be held in his arms this way was much too disconcerting, summoning up memories that were better left unearthed. Just why did he want to dance with her? Certainly the look of abstraction on his face did not give the appearance of one enjoying the waltz.

"How fond are you of your cousin Maria?" he asked abruptly.

"Fond enough," she retorted. "Why do you ask?"

"Because I think if you are fond of her that you should dissuade her from her attachment to Edward Cassidy."

"Edward Cassidy? What have you to say against Edward?"

For a moment he was at *point non plus*. He couldn't accuse Edward of being a rake, not when Eleanor had accepted his own offer three years ago.

He gazed down into her hazel eyes. "All I shall tell you is that I believe Maria would be fatally matched with Edward. He is far too young. And since she is young herself, she might do better with an older husband, one used to the world."

"Someone like you, for instance?" Eleanor said, lifting an eyebrow. "I wouldn't have thought that so noted a Corinthian as yourself would have deemed Edward a rival. Does it smart that Maria prefers him to you."

"My remarks are not motivated by jealousy."

"No? Merely a good deed on your part?" she asked with her eyebrows still arched.

Prescott bit his tongue. He was not known for his good deeds, more's the pity.

"Perhaps you should try to win Maria's hand honestly, instead of resorting to malicious prattle."

"Malicious prattle? I suppose you know Edward's character best?"

"I have observed him with Maria and see him as an honourable young man. Nor have I heard anyone speak against him until you did so just a few minutes ago. Julia, too, speaks highly of him."

"Julia?" Prescott frowned.

"Yes." Eleanor said, watching his mild consternation at the mention of her sister-in-law's name. "And Maria herself dotes on Edward."

"Maria is a silly-headed chit, just like..."

"Just like I was?" she asked, her eyes glinting dangerously.

"No." He had recovered his countenance. "Just like your Aunt Lavinia."

She smiled. "I should have thought you would know my family by now, my lord. Maria may not spurn your advances, but another in my family has hinted you away in the past. And you would be wise to heed her wishes," she said, hoping that he would stay away from Julia.

Prescott looked black. His little talk with Eleanor had not done the thing. And there could be no doubt that she was talking about herself as the one who had hinted him away in the past.

CHAPTER TEN

ELEANOR'S REMOVAL to Cavendish Square was completed later in the week. "Julia was quite insistent that I come the very day that Andrew leaves," she told her mother, "and since he had planned to leave for Wiltshire this morning I'd best go to her now."

"Well, I'll miss you," Lady Constance said, giving her a quick peck, "but I daresay Julia will be glad of your company. I would not confide this to anyone but you, Eleanor, but Julia has been looking a trifle out of sorts these days."

"Do you think so, Mama?" Eleanor asked, wishing her mother were not so acute. "I haven't noticed."

"I daresay you will think I am one of those ticklish females imagining things."

On the contrary Eleanor had a healthy respect for her mother's intuition.

"I do love Julia," Lady Constance said at the door. "She is the perfect wife for Andrew. And you must tell her for me how enchanting she looked in that gown by Fanchon the other night. I wonder why she did not wear the emerald bracelet with the dress."

"Perhaps she preferred a simpler ornament."

"That reminds me, I must ask her to bring over the Whiting brooch. I promised Lavinia that I would show

it to her. She is going to commission something similar.''

"But the ruby brooch is ghastly, Mama," Eleanor
protested.

"Yes, I know, but that won't stop Lavinia from
having it copied.''

A footman passed with Eleanor's portmanteau. She
had packed only the necessities, but even these took up
more room than a valise afforded.

"Now do be sure and let everyone know that I am
with Julia at Cavendish Square. I don't want it
thought I have been packed off in disgrace," Eleanor
teased.

"I suppose it is a rehearsal for what is inevitable,"
Lady Con replied. "You will be leaving for your own
establishment some day. I have been thinking about it
often since Andrew's marriage." She stole a look at
her daughter's face. "Hasn't Harry Addison made
you an offer?''

"Yes," Eleanor admitted.

"Well, don't keep me on tenterhooks. What did you
tell him?''

"I didn't. And please don't hound me about what
my answer will be, for I scarcely know myself. That's
why I'm hoping that at Julia's I will be able to think
the matter through. And I rely on Papa to fob Harry
off.''

"COULDN'T FOB HIM OFF," Sir Donald explained later
in his book room when his daughter came to say her
goodbyes and laid this charge at his door. "Tried to,
that goes without saying, but he cornered me again as
I was coming out of White's. Hated just to cut the

man, so I was obliged to listen to him prattle about how he had lost his heart to you.''

The look of revulsion on his face sparked a gurgle of laughter from his daughter.

"Poor Papa. You should have told him you were not entertaining suitors for me.''

"Bosh! I have an unmarried daughter whom I don't want to marry off? Peculiar sort of father that would make me! Besides, I entertained Prescott's suit, didn't I? And if I could entertain a rake's suit I could entertain one from a dull dog like Addison.''

"Now, Papa, Harry's not that dull,'' Eleanor protested.

Sir Donald put down his copy of the *Racing News*. "It's plain as two pins you don't want him as a husband. Every time I mention his name you wrinkle up your pretty little nose. And when I point out his shortcomings all you can say is, 'Now, Papa.' Three years ago when I mentioned Prescott's shortcomings, you'd fly into a temper and tell me I didn't know what I was talking about. You wanted Prescott then, you don't want Addison now.''

"Must you always bring up Prescott?'' Eleanor demanded, nettled by this accurate reminiscence. "I loathe no one more than him. And as for shortcomings, if you could have heard him last night, advising me to throw a spanner in the works between Edward and Maria, hinting in the most odious way possible about Edward's flaws in order to enlarge his own consequence, and insisting he wasn't playing dog in the manger.''

Sir Donald took off his spectacles. "What did he say about young Edward?''

"Just that he was the wrong match for Maria. Edward warned me earlier that Prescott was saying vile things about him."

"I've never known Prescott to carry tales."

"Always a first time."

"He must be top over tail in love with Maria."

"Yes," Eleanor said, finding no satisfaction in this explanation for his lordship's errant behavior. But if he were in love with Maria, why in heaven was he making advances toward Julia?

AIMÉE HID A DELICATE YAWN behind a hand and wished that Sebastian would finish the canvas he had been working on. For the past week she had sat for him daily and Armand was beginning to become jealous. A smile lifted the corners of her mouth as she remembered some of Armand's words.

"Have you heard any more about your friend? The one who ran away." Aimée asked, as Sebastian consented to a brief respite to enable her to walk her aching limbs about his small atelier.

"Yes," he said, his young face screwed up in dismay. "I have. She is breeding!"

"Ah, worse and worse. Where is she?"

"At a small convent located in Wiltshire. I have it on good authority Isabelle is there. But she won't see me. I've written, and my letters come back unread. I even went out there and had the good sisters slam the door in my face."

"*Très triste.*"

"If I ever find out who put her in that plight, I shall strangle him!" Sebastian said, looking so violent that Aimée hastened to soothe him.

"Strangling him would only bring the law down on your head."

"Mademoiselle Martine, would you help me? Would you go to Wiltshire and speak to Isabelle for me? I don't know whom else to apply to. Most of the females I know are hardly the sort I could dispatch on such a mission. But you are different. I trust you."

Aimée was much touched, but she did not wish to undertake an errand of mercy.

"I think you must be sensible. I don't know your friend. She would hardly believe anything I said."

"Mademoiselle, you must try. I will pay your way to the country. I will write her a letter. You must see that she gets it. That's all I ask. Tell her that I am distraught, that I love her and want to marry her and will raise the babe as my own."

"You would do all that?" Aimée asked, persuaded despite her best intentions to help Sebastian.

"Indeed, yes."

"Then she is a lucky one," Aimée murmured. "Still, how shall I convince the good sisters to let me in?"

Sebastian paced for a moment. "Were you not part of the Comédie Française when you were in Paris? Surely such a good actress should be able to improvise something."

"*Oui,*" she said, her eyes lighting up at the memory of her career on the boards in Paris. "I shall do what you wish. I shall see your little friend. It is all very romantic, is it not?"

It was too romantic to suit Armand when Aimée told him about her trip.

"*Incroyable!* Why do you concern yourself with Sebastian's tiresome affairs?"

Aimée fell silent a moment. When she spoke her tone was pensive. "It could be me, Armand. That is why I said yes to Sebastian. I shall be back so quickly you will never know I have left."

"I shall know," Armand declared. "The hours that you are away will be a penance. If you do not come back I shall kill myself."

Aimée trilled with laughter. "No, you won't. You would find some *jolie fille* to take my place."

He swept her into his arms. "No one could take your place, Aimée," he said, and kissed her.

EDWARD CASSIDY WOKE UP with the most blinding headache he had ever had. He turned over in bed, realizing at once that it was not his bed and he was not alone. He stared down at the strange female next to him. Whoever it was, he couldn't recall her name. He gave her a shake. "Who are you, and where are my breeches?"

"Sally's the name. And your breeches are where you left them on the chair." She sagged back on the dirty pillow.

Edward staggered to the clothes and dressed himself slowly. His head still spun. When he was fully dressed he searched his pockets. Where was his money? Snarling with rage, he shook Sally awake. "Where is my money, you thieving wench?" he demanded.

"There is none."

He slapped her.

"Ow!" she bawled.

"There will be more of that if you don't tell me the truth."

"I am telling you the truth. I don't know where your money is. You didn't give any to me, that much I know. And you still owe me two pounds for last night!"

"How did I get here? How did we meet? Speak!" he threatened.

"Near to two in the morning it was," Sally gulped in fear. "I was out walking and you come along in a carriage and pick me up. You said I looked lucky and would bring you luck at the gaming houses you knew. So we went over there. You played and then we left and came here."

Edward swore. The story seemed only too likely to be true. He had been on top of the world when he had left Almack's, but it was too early to go to bed, so he had made the rounds of the clubs, and must have been heading for the Greeking establishments when he had come across Sally. Good luck, indeed.

It was bad luck she had brought him, he decided as he left her room, blinking in the bright sunlight. He would have to walk home. He sidestepped a few of the urchins in the street and looked so grim that one of them, surveying him in the hopes that he might be an easy mark, thought better of it.

A carriage stopped short next to him. Looking up, he saw Michaels, one of his companions during many a game of whist.

"Up early, Edward," Michaels called down.

"Too early, by half."

"I am on my way home too," Michaels confided. "I shall give you a ride, if you like."

Accepting the offer, Edward climbed up into the seat next to the other gentlemen.

"Foxed?" Michaels asked when Edward winced as the carriage rolled over the cobblestoned street.

Edward forced a laugh. "Just a trifle."

"Well, you were foxed last night when I saw you."

"Oh? You must forgive my abominable memory, Michaels, but did we play last night, the two of us?"

"Oh, no. I was a spectator, the stakes were too high for me." Michaels pursed his lips and whistled admiringly. "But they didn't deter you."

"Just who did I play with?" Edward asked, affecting an air of unconcern when his real wish was to hold his head still with both hands. What in heaven had happened to him last night?

"Rehagen."

"What!" Edward jerked his head up hard. Rehagen wasn't even a gentlemen. He was the most notorious gambler in the city.

"No one else wanted any part of him. But you said let him play. And you were the one with him at the end. How do you figure on paying him off?"

"I lost, then," Edward said.

"My dear Edward, there is not a doubt about that. Close to ten thousand pounds it was. Rehagen gave you a week to pay."

"A week..." All his other debts were nothing compared to the debt to Rehagen. The man would kill him if he didn't pay up. "Michaels, I wonder if you would lend me—"

"Sorry, Edward, my pockets are to let. My uncle keeps me devilishly tight. Papa's fault for that stupid will he left that doesn't give me my inheritance until I'm thirty! What's the point of his dying and leaving me something if I can't enjoy it?"

"Yes," Edward said, the frown on his brow growing more pronounced.

A few minutes later Michaels set him down in front of his quarters. Knowing that he looked hellish, he washed and changed his clothes, but the smell of Sally seemed to linger after his ablutions.

Rehagen. He felt his stomach knot at the name. He might have staved off his other debtors until he had married Maria Whiting and got his hands on her inheritance. But he doubted that he could woo and marry her in a week. Of course he could abduct her and force the marriage. He gave that scheme careful thought but abandoned it as too fraught with problems.

To pay off Rehagen quickly, he must resort to his other plan. He yanked open a drawer of his escritoire and took out a bottle of Dr. Bell's Tonic. It was one of his Uncle Fenley's favourites. He also took out a small bottle of belladonna and poured it into the bottle of tonic. He had been sending his uncle a bottle of tonic a month, with a few drops of belladonna added, but the matter at hand was so urgent, that he could no longer be patient and allow the poison to work its way slowly into his uncle's system. He needed his inheritance within the week.

He sealed the tonic and wrapped it. How fortunate, he reflected, that his uncle was so notorious a hermit that no one would investigate his death. Tucking the parcel under his arm, he set off to post it.

CHAPTER ELEVEN

AIMÉE THOUGHT IT PRUDENT to inform Lord Prescott of her impending absence from London. True, their relationship had dwindled to one of form, but since he still paid the lease on her house and was known to be her patron, she felt it best to tell him. So she dispatched a cream-coloured note to him, asking him to call.

Promptly at two he presented himself at Grosvenor Square where Aimée waited, resplendent in a cerulean-blue walking dress.

"You look ravishing, my dear," he said, taking her hand.

"Not true. I look almost respectable," she replied as he helped her into his phaeton. "I could even pass for that dowdy one, that dragon, Mrs. Burrell, *n'est-ce pas?*"

Prescott chuckled. "Whatever you could pass for, it would not be for Mrs. Drummond Burrell." He flicked the reins lightly and his team of Welshbreds set off. Having Aimée up in the carriage with him sparked memories of other rides together. It seemed like such a long time ago. He frowned as he tried to remember the last time they had enjoyed such an excursion.

"How is your friend Saint Jacques, the painter?" he asked.

"He is very well. He painted a landscape the other day that fetched a hundred pounds. They say that the Regent himself was interested in buying it for his collection."

"Well, if so, I'd advise Armand to ask for the money straight out. Prinny is notoriously purse-pinched, if you believe what is said."

"The Regent has never cheated any artist. Indeed they say he often takes young ones under his wing and provides them with much-needed funds."

"A patron of the arts, that's Prinny," Prescott agreed. They had reached the entrance to the Park, and his highsteppers led the way in. "Do I deduce Prinny's hand behind your note?" he asked.

"How you love to jest, Prescott. I have nothing to do with the Regent, as well you know. I shall be leaving London on a private matter for a while and thought I should tell you so."

"My dear Aimée, such a civility must please."

Aimée's rich laughter bubbled out. "You do pay the lease on my house," she reminded him.

"Where are you off to? Or is this a rendezvous with Armand?"

"*Non.* Armand remains in London."

"Not another friend waiting in the wings?" he quizzed. It wasn't Aimée's style to have two lovers when one would do.

"*Mon Dieu, non.* Armand is jealous enough of you, he would be twice as jealous of another. He is even jealous of Sebastian, the painter I am sitting for this week. It is on Sebastian's account that I am going to the dreary Wiltshire," she revealed and quickly confided the story about the painter and his love.

"An errand of mercy, Aimée?" He chuckled.

To his surprise she took exception to his innocent words. "It is easy for you to laugh at the poor child..."

"Heavens, I wasn't laughing," he protested but she went on without a pause.

"...but it could be me in her situation."

"Impossible."

She shifted her weight on the carriage seat. "By-blows are nothing unusual in your society, my lord."

He was silent as the Welshbreds made a turn toward the Serpentine.

"Had I had a child, Prescott, you would not have married me," Aimée went on softly.

"Marriage would have been out of the question," he acknowledged. "But I would not have abandoned you," he said.

A ghost of a smile touched her lips. "You would have set me up in a fine establishment," she agreed. "And even educated the babe. But you would not have legitimized him."

Prescott began to chafe under this rebuke, before realizing that he was suffering pangs of guilt over a situation that had not occurred.

"I don't see why we are talking of this," he expostulated. "You speak as though our child were here. It is not. Unless," he said, darting a quick and worried look her way, "this is your way of broaching the news of its existence to me."

Aimée erupted into a gurgle of laughter. "*Mon Dieu, non*. But if you could see your face."

"Then let us return to the point of your leaving for Wiltshire," he said agreeably. "Do you have enough funds for the trip?"

"Yes, I believe so. There are some pressing bills from Fanchon."

"You should have had them direct it to me as usual," Prescott said promptly.

"I did not like to do so. Our relationship is not what it used to be. I did not want to take advantage of your generosity."

He brought his team to a halt and turned to cup her chin. "You are a rare female, Aimée. I see why I fell in love with you."

"That was years ago," she said, smiling at the memory. "You were very green."

"I should be jealous of Armand."

"But you are not. And I know why. You are wearing the willow for Eleanor Whiting."

If anyone else had uttered these words Lord Prescott would have throttled him, but Aimée knew him only too well.

"Send Fanchon's bill to me at once." He said brusquely, ignoring the comment. "How do you plan to get to this convent?"

"By Mail Coach."

He grimaced. "You don't wish to be racketed about the kingdom in a Mail Coach, squeezed in between a fat farmer's wife and a lecherous clerk. I have a travel chaise that I shall put at your disposal. My groom will drive you to Wiltshire and back."

"Prescott—" Aimée protested.

"Do you want to be pinched at in a Mail Coach or posting house?"

"Well, no," she said.

"Then it is settled. Though I must vow that the idea of your playing Cupid and bringing Sebastian and his young friend together again does boggle my mind."

"Armand was of the same opinion. It is very romantic, *n'est-ce pas?*"

"Very," he agreed. "You love Armand, don't you, Aimée?"

"Oui."

"Good," he said. "Good."

She gave his arm a squeeze as he started the carriage off again, a move that was not lost on some of the others observing him, including Maria Whiting and Edward Cassidy.

The couple had taken their own turn around the Serpentine, with Edward waiting for the chance to pop the question. The sight of Prescott's carriage, however, had made him change his plans. He slowed his team into a veritable crawl, explaining to his companion that he did not wish the drive to be over too soon.

"Isn't that Lord Prescott's carriage ahead?" she asked.

"Oh, so it is."

"Who is that female in the carriage?"

"That is his *chère amie*, Aimée Martine."

"Really?" Maria said. "Do you mean he rides with her?"

"Among other things. He practically flaunted her in the face of your cousin three years ago, which is why she broke off their match. Did you not know?"

"No," Maria murmured. "She is very beautiful."

"You cast her in the shade," Edward said. "I hope you have not been too distressed at seeing her with Prescott. I know your liking of him."

"Oh I am not distressed," Maria declared. "I do like him, but I like you better. His lordship can be so daunting at times. When he asks me a question, I sometimes tremble lest I give the wrong answer."

"Yes, he can be rather a bear at times. He once thundered at me for some trifle, as though he himself hadn't kicked up larks in the past. An unforgiving sort of person, Prescott."

"Then do take the other road," Maria urged, "so we needn't cross his path."

The rest of the carriage ride passed agreeably enough, and Edward returned Maria to Lady Vyne's and started back to his own residence. No sooner had he stepped out his carriage than he felt his arm grabbed and twisted behind his back. Pain shot up through him like a knife.

"Don't cry out, guv'nor," a voice hissed in his ear as he was hastily forced back into his carriage.

"My arm! Don't break it."

"I'd sooner break an arm than a neck," came the sneering reply as Edward fell into the carriage. He faced his assailant and swallowed hard. The man looked all of six foot with a black beard and a broken nose. "My employer is annoyed with the likes of you. You be owing him money. He sent me round to remind you of it."

"I don't need a reminder. I shall have it for him in a week's time. He'll have to be patient."

"Perhaps you'd like to tell that to Mr. Rehagen himself."

"No," Edward said quickly. He had no wish to face Rehagen again. "I shall have the money by the end of the week."

The bearded man glared at him in silence.

"He'll get nothing from a dead man."

The other man snorted.

"I'll have all of it. Ten thousand pounds, I swear."

There was a chuckle. "You be forgetting the interest that's due."

"He'll have the interest too. Everything, I swear. By week's end."

"I'll tell Rehagen. He may believe you, and he may not. In any case don't get too attached to this arm, guv'nor," he said and left the carriage. Edward sat back weakly, nursing his arm.

AT CAVENDISH SQUARE Eleanor was settling into the room that Julia had prepared for her. A cheerful blue chamber with chubby cherubs staring from the ceiling, it put her in mind of her old room when she was a child.

"I will only stay until Andrew returns," Eleanor said. "I should hate to have anyone think that he has taken his spinster sister under his protection!"

"Spinster!" Julia choked. "Oh, you are funning. Who would dare to say such a thing."

"Lady Sonnings."

"Oh, she's just an odious prattlebox. And I know why she says hateful things. It's because her daughter is making her come-out this year. A simpering miss if I ever saw one," Julia declared.

A footman arrived with the portmanteau, and the two ladies set to work shaking out Eleanor's dresses.

"Good, this one hasn't got too crushed," Eleanor said examining an apricot silk. "I plan to wear it to Lady Fogarty's musicale tonight."

"Come and see what I am wearing," Julia coaxed and led the way into her room. The gold-coloured silk would complement Julia's hair to perfection.

"It's beautiful," Eleanor murmured.

"And I am wearing this with it," Julia said, pointing to a new gold bracelet on her dressing table. "A gift from Andrew before he left."

"Good heavens, my brother is a romantic."

"Yes, he's the dearest man."

Eleanor tried on the bracelet and held it up to the sunlight to admire. For some reason her sister-in-law did not appear as delighted with the gift as she would have ordinarily. She unclasped the bracelet and handed it back to Julia.

The jewellery reminded Eleanor of Lady Constance's request for the Whiting brooch, and she put the request to Julia now.

"What Whiting brooch?" Julia asked, nearly catching her finger in her jewel box.

Eleanor laughed. "There's only the one, large and hideous and studded with rubies in the shape of a spider."

"Why does your aunt want it?"

"Something about commissioning a similar piece, I believe. You know Aunt Lavinia's freakish whims."

"Yes," Julia said, thinking frantically.

Eleanor was always so understanding. She had understood about Prescott and about her gaming debts, but would she understand the pawning of a family heirloom? She and Andrew both shared the family pride in the Whiting name. They would not countenance having the Whiting brooch sold to pay for gaming debts.

"Julia? You look to be in a brown study, my dear," Eleanor's soft laugh tinkled.

"Oh, I beg pardon, Eleanor. I've just been trying to think of the brooch. And now I recall that the clasp came loose and so I sent it out to be repaired. I hope Aunt Lavinia is not in too much of a hurry to see it.''

"Oh, I daresay Aunt Lavinia can wait. Although I think that one hideous brooch in our family is enough. Perhaps she will come to her senses and commission something else.''

"I pray she will,'' Julia said sincerely, and then, recalled to her duties as a hostess by her guest's remark that she was hungry enough to eat a bear, took her off to enjoy their customary cup of tea.

WHILE JULIA AND EDWARD both rued the gaming habits that had brought them to their present perilous situations, Lord Prescott returned home to Berkeley Square and ordered his groom to accompany Aimée on her journey to Wiltshire.

"Very good, my lord,'' Walter said woodenly, though it was apparent by the stiff set to his jaw that he was not too pleased.

Prescott laid his gloves and cane on the ormolu table. "Aimée is a very good friend, Walter, I am entrusting her to your care.''

"I'll be driving her down the way you ordered me to,'' the groom said stiffly.

"And help her over any unpleasantness if there is any,'' Prescott added.

Walter bit his lip. "Yes, my lord.''

"Good. Thank you, Walter.''

Walter was not the only one in the household to look askance at the idea of Prescott sending his travel chaise to his chère amie. But although the servants buzzed to themselves they did not question their employer.

Lord Prescott did not concern himself with such thoughts. He sat down in his library, thinking back to the ride in the Park with her. It had been a comfortable, friendly ride. That was how he thought of Aimée these days, a friend instead of a lover. And he had ruefully to admit that was how Aimée thought of him. She had Armand now, the impetuous Frenchman who, Prescott often thought, would have run a sword through him if Aimée had not dissuaded him. Aimée did love Armand. Armand, he knew, was always beseeching her to marry him, something she would not do until he had the money to afford her.

Even in love, Aimée kept her head. Prescott got up from his chair. Armand was an artist, and such fellows had notoriously poor incomes unless they attracted the notice of a patron who would supply them with a regular allowance. So far Armand had failed to attract such notice. Unless... An idea began to kindle in Prescott's brain, one which after ten minutes of furious thought he was obliged to admit was the nackiest notion he had ever dreamed up and which he took quick steps to put into action.

CHAPTER TWELVE

LADY FOGARTY'S MUSICALE was a high point of the London Season, and many young ladies practised their scales diligently for the weeks leading up to the great event.

Eleanor was the exception, for she boasted no abilities with musical instruments, having tried the patience of three music masters who had attempted to teach her the piano, violin and harp. Julia, however, had already agreed to play at the musicale, so Eleanor cheerfully accepted her duty to accompany her sister-in-law there. Harry Addison had generously volunteered his escort, although he was, as he confessed during the carriage ride, wholly tone deaf.

"That might be a blessing," Eleanor said, settling back against the velvet squabs. "Do you remember the poor girl who became unhinged when she flung her bow into the audience while playing her violin?"

"Yes, but it ended happily," Julia reminded her, "for the bow landed in the lap of Lord Jeld whom she was trying to attract. And an announcement in the *Morning Post* followed within the month."

"Well, I do hope other marriage-minded females will not adopt that tactic," Eleanor said, picturing a variety of instruments landing in a succession of male laps. "What are you playing tonight?"

"Bach," Julia replied nervously. "I do hope it will serve."

Eleanor patted her arm reassuringly.

Their arrival at the Palladian residence of the Fogartys coincided with that of the majority of guests, and they were forced to cool their heels until the crush had cleared.

As they made their way through the corniched doorway, several other guests smiled and nodded greetings, among them Mr. Thomas Rose, carrying his bugle.

"Good heavens, he's not going to play that, is he?" Eleanor asked.

"Zounds, I hope not," Harry said fervently. "He used to be in the cavalry."

Together they climbed up the Adam stairway and soon were being greeted by their hostess dressed in a stunning lavender-and-white dress with matching mauve kid gloves.

"Oh my dear Miss Whiting," Lady Fogarty seized on Julia in an excess of emotion, "such a commotion has arisen. And you are the one who can save us."

"Really, Lady Fogarty?"

"Would you mind going first on the programme?" Lady Fogarty asked. "I know you were to be third, but Miss Tymes slipped this morning and broke her right arm and is quite unable to ply that harp. She is most distraught over it.

"The piano is in the music room. I told them to put your music first, hoping you would consent. Do go and get it all prepared, won't you?" She fanned herself and her heaving double chins.

While Julia busied herself with the music sheets in the music room, Harry strolled to a small harp that occupied a corner and gave one of the strings a pluck.

"If you do that I shall tell Lady Fogarty that you will ply the harp in place of Miss Tymes," Eleanor warned.

Harry laughed. "I say, here comes your cousin Maria. Is she to perform this evening?"

Maria, they soon discovered, was indeed performing on the flute, an instrument she had been schooled in for the past two years.

"But I had no idea it would be such a vast audience," she confessed to Eleanor.

"You needn't be fearful. We will cheer you on," she said soothingly.

"By Jove, yes," Harry said. "I am looking forward to the piece. Is that the flute you will play?"

"Yes." Maria handed it to him.

He fingered it gingerly. "You must be very talented."

"Well, it's all in the way you breathe."

"Then your breathing must be devilishly talented," Harry said, and looked bewildered when they all laughed.

Owing to bouts of stage fright as well as Miss Tymes's accident, the program had to be abruptly revised and Julia led off on the pianoforte, playing a splendid Bach and earning a round of applause for her efforts.

Maria followed on the flute with a trio of sprightly Scottish songs that also won the approval of the audience. Unfortunately the same could not be said of Mr. Rose who did indeed play his bugle, causing Eleanor to rue the fact that she was seated so close to the front of the room. The music emanating from Mr. Rose put an end to all conversation and one could almost hear the thundering hooves of the cavalry on the charge.

Despite the noise of the bugle, Harry Addison attempted to put a question to her, one she was obliged to ask him to repeat twice, both times without being able to deduce what he was saying.

"You must speak up, Harry," she said.

"I said are you going to marry me?" he thundered, just as Mr. Rose brought the bugle down from his lips.

Silence covered the room as Eleanor blushed, well aware that Harry had given the quizzes something to gossip about. Fortunately Diana, seeing her predicament, began to clap for the hapless Mr. Rose, and soon others joined in.

The rest of the musicale went on as scheduled and without incident except for Miss Chartredge's forgetting the lyrics of the song she was singing, and staying an agonised eternity at high C until her memory was dislodged by her mother who hissed the forgotten words from the back of the room.

Diana and Philip were slated to bring the musicale to a close with a duet, a series of love songs, but Philip Hawthorne had come down with a sore throat, so she was in need of a partner. Lady Fogarty appealed to her audience. Of the gentlemen present few of them were of the performing inclination and a good many others were like Harry, tone deaf.

"Lord Prescott will do it," Mrs. Edgewater said, nudging her nephew in the ribs, much to his stupefaction.

"Oh thank you, Lord Prescott," Lady Fogarty beamed.

The next few minutes were a penance for his lordship, who wondered what had induced his aunt to volunteer him. Fortunately Diana had brought the music and words to her songs to the front of the room, and he was able to follow along. A spirited burst of applause rewarded their efforts.

"There is one other song," Diana said now. "But I fear that I have overtasked my voice so I beg your leave to persuade my friend Eleanor Whiting to take my place. Eleanor?" she entreated.

Eleanor stared dumbfounded at her. What could Diana be thinking? Furiously she shook her head.

"Come, come Miss Whiting. Where is your sense of good sportsmanship?" Prescott asked, his eyes glinting with mischief. "Which song is it to be, Mrs. Hawthorne?"

"This one," Diana gave him a sheaf of papers. "Do study it, Prescott. And I wouldn't ask, Eleanor, but my throat is sore and it's a surprise for you."

"A surprise?"

"Look."

Grinning, Diana held out the music sheets. Scanning them, Eleanor recognized the lyrics as her own.

"I put your poem to music," Diana said. "I will play the piano myself. You can't say no."

Well aware that Diana's gift meant much to her, Eleanor saw no way out of singing the duet with Lord Prescott.

"Courage, Miss Whiting," he said, strolling over. "I'd advise you to inhale deeply, singing is just so much breathing, you know," he said and began his part in the song.

Standing next to him, staring at the sheet in front of her, Eleanor did not have to listen very hard. She knew each word by heart, having written them when she was in love with him years ago.

He paused, and she sang her words.

"Always, I will love you, not once or twice, but always," she sang her part and he joined her for the chorus.

"Always, I will love you."

Finally, their voices were stilled at the song's conclusion, and then there was vociferous applause.

He bent down and saw that her hands were shaking.

"That wasn't so bad, was it?" he asked, picking one up. "All in all, a pretty little song, wouldn't you say?"

Eleanor felt uncharacteristically tongue-tied. His eyes were fixed on the pulse beating in her throat. Then Harry strolled up to compliment her.

"Harry, my throat is parched, will you escort me to the refreshment room please?" With a quick bow, she made her escape.

Prescott remembered Harry's booming question of a few minutes ago. Just when would Eleanor be marrying Addison?

"Thank you for you assistance, my lord," Diana said to Prescott as she gathered her music sheets.

"It was my pleasure," Prescott said. "Did you write the song yourself?"

"I composed the music," she admitted with shy pride.

"My congratulations. And the lyrics? They were so poignant."

She sent him a sidelong look. "I didn't write them. Eleanor did."

"Miss Whiting?"

"Yes. It's quite good, don't you think? The emotion is very powerful."

"Indeed yes," Prescott said, rather grimly. Apparently Eleanor's feeling for Harry Addison ran deeper than he had thought. She had even written love poems about the chap.

WHILE HARRY WAS TRYING to snare Eleanor her share of the lobster patties, Julia was attempting to find a way to speak to Edward Cassidy, who was among the late arrivals at the musicale. As befitted one in the throes of a grand passion, Edward was hanging on Maria's every word. But at last Julia saw her chance and drew Edward aside for a moment.

"Mr. Cassidy, I am obliged to ask for your help once again. It's my brooch—the one you sold for me the other day."

"Oh?" he asked, wondering if she had learned that Grimes had paid twice what he had told her.

"I must have it back. It's an heirloom. Please, Mr. Cassidy, won't you help me get it back?"

"Do you have the money to get it back?" he countered.

"I have three hundred pounds. And I'll give him this ring." She was holding out her hand. "It was my mother's. It should be worth seven hundred pounds."

"Perhaps," Edward agreed. "But he might not sell it back for a thousand pounds."

"Why not? That's what he paid me for it!"

"Er, yes, very true. But some of these sellers are very unscrupulous. They know that a lady is attached to her jewellery and so they increase the price she must pay."

"Increase it how much?"

"Sometimes as much as twice."

Julia's face fell. "But I can't pay that much."

"I will see and ask him. Perhaps I can persuade him to take these items. But he may want more."

"Oh thank you," Julia said. "Thank you. You are so good to help me this way."

"Always pleased to help a relation of Maria's," Edward said, putting her ring in his pocket.

Julia walked quickly away from Edward, her mind still in a tumult. Vaguely she became aware that Lord Prescott was watching her. She repressed a shiver as he came toward her with a glass of champagne.

"Would you care for a glass of champagne, Mrs. Whiting?" he asked now. "I find myself with two."

Was he trying to get her foxed, the better to aid his plans of seduction?

"No, thank you," she said.

He placed one of the glasses on the tray and sipped the other. "I couldn't help but notice you and Edward speaking together. I advise you to be cautious in dealing with him."

"Cautious!" Julia's eyes widened. Was Prescott now threatening to tell Andrew about her friendship with Edward? Would he twist this harmless relationship into something more sinister, perhaps to allow him his way with her?

"If you will allow me to pass, my lord," she said coldly and with her back rigid she left the room.

Chatting nearby with Diana, Eleanor had not missed the exchange between Prescott and Julia. Was he still set on pursuing Julia? For a minute she felt a pang. Hearing him sing her own words of love to her had triggered the most contradictory emotions in her breast, emotions she had stifled years ago. Would that he had been singing them in truth!

But what was she thinking of? Lord Prescott was a hardened rake. He had proved that three years ago and was proving it anew in his pursuit of Julia.

"Eleanor, have you been listening to a word I've been saying?" Diana asked laughing.

Eleanor glanced up, as her friend shook her head in amusement.

"I was asking if you would accompany me tomorrow while I sit for my portrait?"

"I don't see why you will need me," Eleanor said.

"Well, you know the reputation of some of these artists. And Philip says if you go with me he will rest easier."

"If such is the case, have the artist come to your residence."

"It wouldn't be the same." Diana nibbled on a sweetmeat. "Besides, I should have to worry about him spilling his paints and ruining my Wilton or perhaps callers coming unexpectedly. No, it's much better to go there, except that I shall need someone to accompany me. Say you will go, Eleanor."

"What is the painter's name?"

"Armand Saint Jacques. Have you heard of him?"

Eleanor shook her head.

"They say he is very good. He's French, of course, which is why Philip is doubly anxious that I have someone with me."

"Then you may tell Philip his fears are in vain. I shall be your chaperon."

"Thank you, Eleanor." Diana squeezed her hand. "You are the best of friends. And who knows perhaps you will decide to have your portrait painted too."

The rest of the evening drifted by, and it was only later when Eleanor was ready to go home that she realized she had not seen Julia since her stormy tête-à-tête with Lord Prescott. She conducted a swift search of the rooms, stopping in the hallway when she saw his lordship coming toward her. She had been avoiding him ever since the duet foisted on her by Diana.

"If you are looking for Addison he is in the middle of a rousing discussion on the care and feeding of Arabians."

She stifled a laugh. "Really, my lord..."

"I'm telling you the truth. What is it to be, yes or no?"

"Yes or no?" she asked, put wholly at sea by his question.

His dark eyes were unfathomable pools. "About Addison's proposal. He declared himself in a room full of people. Even my aunt is bursting to know. I daresay the columns of both the *Morning Post* and the *Gazette* will include it in the on-dits tomorrow. To cut the quizzes short, I'd advise you to have your decision ready. You can send in the announcement to the *Gazette* and clinch the matter."

"Thank you for the advice, my lord," she said in dulcet tones. "And now perhaps you could advise me of Julia's whereabouts."

"As a matter of fact, yes," he replied blandly. "I saw her in the card room."

"The card room?" Eleanor paled and hurried off, not appearing to notice that Prescott was accompanying her. She immediately spotted Julia seated at a far table. Her sister-in-law's face was flushed and from her laughter it was apparent that she was winning.

"She's had a run of good luck." Prescott bent slightly toward her. "Unfortunately that will not last. I'd suggest you take her home and see that she stays there."

Although this was the very stratagem that Eleanor intended to adopt, she did not like his interference in family matters.

"Julia is not your concern, my lord," she said scorchingly. "I wish you would remember that."

He drew back. "Would you rather see her in a debtor's prison?"

"No, of course not."

"Then stop being so gooseish and take her home where she belongs," he ordered and turned on his heel.

He was odious and insufferable—and right, about Julia at least, Eleanor acknowledged. That made her even more furious at him. Quickly, she overrode Julia's protests and separated her from the table, then bundled her off into their carriage for the ride back to Cavendish Square.

CHAPTER THIRTEEN

"I THOUGHT that you were not to gamble any more, Julia," Eleanor said the next morning.

"But I won, Eleanor, I won," Julia exclaimed as she arranged a bouquet of red roses in a vase. "Don't you see what a difference that makes? I would have stopped gambling if I had been losing, but since I was winning, it would have been silly not to have continued."

Eleanor sighed, and her head of copper-coloured curls shook slightly.

"Julia, you are already sunk into debt. Surely it is folly to tempt fate further."

"But luck can change, as mine did last night," Julia replied, her words tumbling after each other in her excitement. Her face was lit with joy at finally breaking her unlucky streak. "As it is I won nearly enough for the brooch—" she bit her tongue. Too late.

"What brooch?" Eleanor asked absently sniffing a rosebud.

"For the repair of the brooch, I mean," Julia amended swiftly. "And I promise to quit the next time if I start to lose."

Feeling that this was the best promise she could extract from Julia for the present, Eleanor said no more, and turned her thoughts to her visit with Diana to the painter Armand later that morning.

AT THE AGREED-UPON TIME of ten o'clock, Diana
called for Eleanor, and the two ladies were just stepping down the steps toward their carriage when a familiar high-perched phaeton entered Cavendish
Square.

Eleanor spoke in an urgent undertone to her companion. "Delay our departure a moment, Diana."

Diana shot her a questioning look which changed to
one of comprehension when she observed Prescott's
vehicle drawing up on the flagway. "It's Lord Prescott," she said.

"Yes," Eleanor said, looking grim. "And I will
send him about his business forthwith."

His lordship had spent a restless night, tossing and
turning on his great four-poster, unable to get the image of Eleanor out of his mind. They had sung those
words of love together, words she had written for
Harry Addison.

The thought that she was seriously in love with Addison and might even marry him had jarred him
enough to seek her out today. He could not keep dissembling. He was still in love with Eleanor. He had
never stopped loving her in the three years that they
had not spoken. He would speak his piece and if she
still wanted Addison, so be it.

Accordingly, upon rising, he had gone straight off
to Mount Street, only to find Sir Donald and Lady
Constance, but no sign of Eleanor. He had learned
that Eleanor was staying with Julia Whiting. This was
an unforeseen obstacle since Mrs. Whiting, for reasons which fully escaped Prescott, seemed to have
taken him in a profound dislike.

But now Eleanor was standing in front of him, looking quite beautiful in a blue walking dress hemmed in gold.

"Good morning, Miss Whiting," he said, directing a dazzling smile at her and an equally dazzling one at Diana.

"Good morning," Eleanor returned coolly, affected more than she liked to think by his smile.

"On your way out?" he enquired.

"Not quite," Eleanor replied. If he thought that he had a clear path to Julia he was wholly mistaken. She would bar the door to him if need be.

"Eleanor has agreed to accompany me to a portrait sitting," Diana volunteered.

"Miss Whiting, may I have a word with you, privately? You will excuse us, I hope, Mrs. Hawthorne?"

Consenting to this request, Eleanor walked with him toward his vehicle.

Prescott faced her. This was hardly the romantic moment he had envisioned, with Diana watching covertly from the carriage and the coaches passing on the street.

"This is deuced awkward," he said finally, turning his great beaver around in his hands.

"I daresay it is," Eleanor agreed drily. A man bent on seducing another man's wife would own to some qualms at confronting her sister-in-law.

"How long do you plan to stay with Mrs. Whiting?"

Long enough to scotch your plans, my lord, she yearned to say, but now merely informed him that she would remain at Cavendish Square until Andrew's return.

"You are a diligent companion to your sister-in-law," he said.

Was that a note of vexation in his voice? "I try to be, my lord," she said. "And I daresay we need not peel eggs between the two of us. I'm afraid that you are wasting your time. There is no point to your calling today or at any future time. I am resolved on that with all my heart."

"Will you not allow me to speak my piece—" he protested.

"No," she said at once. "You are so charming a suitor, Lord Prescott, that any female would find herself hoodwinked by your declarations of love. It is better to forestall them now, before irreparable harm is done."

With the greatest effort Prescott held himself in check. He felt close to throttling her or, what was worse, seizing her in his arms and kissing her senseless.

"I wish I could change your mind." Was it so difficult for her to forget what had happened three years ago?

"You cannot," she said. "You'd best go."

A muscle worked in his jaw. "That is your final word on this topic?"

"Yes," she said, a little frightened by the emotion in his dark eyes.

"Very well." He clapped his hat back onto his head, picked up her hand and pressed it to his lips.

A flame seemed to leap from her hand up the entire length of her arm and into her heart. Then he climbed into his carriage and drove away without looking back.

She glanced down at her hand, amazed that there was no scorch mark from where his lips had branded her.

Eleanor was still in a daze when Diana came toward her. "What was that all about?"

"Nothing that signifies," Eleanor said, rubbing the spot on her hand where he had kissed it.

Being a wise friend, Diana did not press her. They reached Armand's studio, and Diana was soon seated on a stool and her profile examined. Armand declared that she was blessed with such excellent features that both profiles were distinguished.

"I shall paint first the right and then the left," he declared authoritatively.

"Not in the same painting, now," Diana protested. "Philip will think that odd."

"No, no. First I start with the full face. Then the next painting will be the right profile and then the left."

"But I only want the one painting."

"Madame, once you see the paintings, you will want them all, and those you do not want I can always sell."

"Who would buy a portrait of me?"

"Many, once they know I painted it," Armand boasted. He set to work applying paint to his palette, and Eleanor amused herself by going through his sketches and the canvases drying on the wall. Armand did have talent, she realized after a brief turn round his studio.

While he painted, Armand chattered about the Regent and how Prinny had taken several painters under his wing and how their paintings had gone up in value accordingly.

"Have you sold him anything, Monsieur Armand?" Diana asked.

A look of regret touched the artist's face. "Not yet," he admitted ruefully. "But I have hopes. I have been approached by someone quite interested in buying my work. An anonymous buyer. I think it could be the Regent himself. And if he likes my work, others will follow."

"How fortunate for you," Eleanor murmured. She had finished with a stack of canvases against one wall and methodically began on another stack. She stopped when she came across a painting of a woman in a field. The landscape was striking, particularly because of the woman with high cheekbones and a sunny complexion.

Eleanor did not need to look twice at the woman. It was a picture of Aimée Martine. Through the haze of memory she recalled that Aimée was a painter's model in addition to her other talents.

She certainly seemed to be a favourite model of Armand, for she reappeared in many more of his paintings, sometimes in the background, sometimes prominently in the fore. In all of them the painter took pains to show her at her best. She would not have been surprised to learn Armand was in love with her, too.

"I see you are admiring my paintings of Aimée." The painter spoke from his easel. He was wiping off his brush, having given in to Diana's urgent request for a brief halt so that she might ease the crick in her neck.

"You have done many paintings of her?"

"I would do all my paintings of her if I could," Armand declared. "Unfortunately she is much in demand by other artists."

"Perhaps I should thank my stars for that or I would not be sitting for my portrait today." Diana suggested, stretching her aching back.

"Madame, I did not mean to imply that I am anything but enchanted to paint you," Armand said hastily. "Besides, Aimée is not available today, nor will she be any time soon." He went back to mixing his paints. "She is too generous and has too much sympathy for the men in her life. She can be taken advantage of. That is why she must needs go off to that convent."

"Convent?" Eleanor's eyes widened. "Has she decided to take orders then, Monsieur Armand?"

"*Non!* She goes for a visit. It is a convent where the young unmarried ladies who are—" he paused delicately "—a tiny bit *enceinte* go to be cared for until the arrival of their babies."

"Oh dear," Diana ejaculated, darting a quick look at Eleanor whose face was drained of colour. "Armand, this Aimée is she not the one who enjoys the patronage of Lord Prescott?"

"*Mais oui.* That is she," Armand said. "This Prescott. I would strangle him if she would let me. But no, she is full of soft words for him. He even lent her the use of his travel chaise to go to the country. Such an understanding gentleman."

"Indeed," Eleanor said woodenly. She turned again to the stack of canvases in front of her, but their vibrant colours seemed to mock her. Prescott's chère amie was increasing and had been sent to a convent to have his child!

DIANA CHATTERED ON about everything but Prescott to Eleanor during their carriage ride home. Perhaps it was the chatter of her well-meaning friend or just the jarring of the carriage wheels over the cobblestoned road, but Eleanor soon found herself with a blinding headache.

"Will you be attending Vauxhall on Friday?" Diana asked. "They say the fireworks are the best ever."

"They always say that," Eleanor laughed. "And it is always the same. Some things never change." Her face sobered. "Just as some men don't."

Diana gave up all attempt at normal conversation, leaning across to squeeze Eleanor's hand.

"I know what you must be feeling. Prescott with a by-blow! Good heavens, who would have thought it!"

Eleanor emitted a bitter laugh. "Good heavens, Di, we are not schoolroom misses. We shouldn't be so shocked. He is a rake. What more does one expect from a rake than to produce such offspring." She paused. "I am so grateful I had the foresight to break off our engagement. I might be married to him now and faced with this situation. Imagine sending his light o'love to that convent in his own travel chaise, flaunting his deed before the world. Unforgivable! Oh, he looks charming and handsome, but he is beyond contempt. Particularly in the way he treats women. I speak not only from my own experience but that of Aimée and Julia."

"Julia?" Diana's eyebrows rose. "Good heavens, he hasn't . . ."

"No," Eleanor said hastily, "but it's not from lack of trying. Julia has been attempting to fend him off, and today I bluntly told him to leave her alone."

"Good for you. But what about Maria? He also seems most interested in her."

"Yes, I know," Eleanor said, troubled deeply by the idea of young, innocent Maria in Lord Prescott's clutches.

THE ONLY CLUTCHES Maria found herself in at the moment were those of Edward Cassidy. A second after she had submitted to what she considered to be the most dizzying kiss she had ever received on her chaste lips, she drew away.

"Maria," Edward begged. "Do put me out of my wretched misery and tell me that you will marry me."

"Of course I shall marry you," Maria said recklessly, abandoning herself to another embrace by her ardent suitor.

Edward had caught her unawares as she sat at the piano playing for him, but she had to admit that no one was as strikingly good-looking as he was, and no one had ever kissed her in that fashion. She had been sent to London to make a match. Her Aunt Lavinia fully approved of Edward, so it seemed idiotish to continue to keep him dangling.

Scarcely believing his good luck, Edward planted another kiss on Maria's lips, this one a trifle more bruising than the last.

"We must tell your aunt," he said huskily.

Lady Vyne's reaction was everything Maria could have wanted.

"Careful, Aunt," she felt obliged to warn, "you must not get too excited or you will have one of your spasms."

"Oh, botheration!" Lady Vyne replied, a statement which would have greatly astonished everyone residing under her roof, since she was wholly addicted to her spasms. "Do tell me everything. Ed-

ward, you cannot find a lovelier, sweeter child in all
England."

"Well do I know that," Edward said, squeezing
Maria's hand. "I only hope her father approves of the
match."

"I shall write him straight away. Oh, there is so
much to discuss, the wedding plans, the announcement to the *Gazette*, your wedding clothes."

"Dowry," Edward added in a teasing way. "One
mustn't forget the dowry, now."

Maria exchanged a meaningful look with her aunt.
"As to that, Edward..." she began primly.

"We shan't forget that, Edward," Lady Vyne said,
directing a baleful eye at her niece. "The flowers for
the wedding, the invitations. Oh, I shall be up to my
neck in the arrangements. Oh, Edward, I could not
welcome you more into our family!"

The sincerity of this remark was proved in the next
instant as Lavinia delved into her favorite topic of the
family tree, insisting that the sprigs which would
sprout from Edward and Maria's branch were bound
to be the best of the lot. Maria blushed while Edward
wondered how long the prattle would continue and
when they would let him know Maria's precise inheritance.

Midway through their discussion a diversion arrived in the person of Lord Prescott, coming to invite
Maria for a ride in the Park.

"Oh, good heavens, Lord Prescott," Maria apologized quickly. "I can't. Not that I am not sensible of
the honour, for I am. But Mr. Cassidy here has just
offered for me and I have accepted him, and so..."

"And so there can be no drives in the Park with any
other gentlemen," Edward put in.

"Quite understandable," Prescott said. "Am I then to wish you happy?" he asked Maria.

"Yes," Maria said with a pretty smile.

"No hard feelings, Prescott, I hope?" Edward asked, holding out his hand.

"None in the least," Lord Prescott said coolly; nonetheless he turned and ignored Edward's outstretched hand.

CHAPTER FOURTEEN

LAVINIA HAD ALLOWED no grass to grow under her feet and had immediately made for Mount Street to share the news of Maria's successful match. Lady Constance suffered through the tale of Edward and Maria's courtship until Lavinia got to Lord Prescott's stormy exit.

She had noticed Prescott favouring Maria with his attentions. Only a ninnyhammer like Lavinia, reflected Lady Constance, would think he had been seriously dangling after the chit. The indolent way he smiled at her was nothing like the way he had courted Eleanor three years ago.

"I do think Edward is just the young man for her, don't you agree?" Lavinia asked, peering into the box of bonbons Lady Constance proffered.

"Perhaps."

Lady Vyne looked startled and drew back her hand. "Do you have some objections to him?" she demanded.

"I have heard that Edward's estates are badly mortgaged."

"So are many estates in England," Lavinia countered, defensively. "And since when have you listened to on-dits?"

"It was Donald who told me this," Lady Constance replied.

"Well, he must have been listening to gossip. Edward told me that he was very plump in the pocket."

"I also recall that you told him that Maria was an heiress," Lady Constance said, snipping the thread off her embroidery. "Or have you finally disabused him of that notion?"

"Not yet. I mean to," Lady Vyne promised, squirming momentarily under the august eye of her sister-in-law.

"AND OF COURSE she will do no such thing," Lady Constance informed her husband upon his return from White's.

"So it's to be young Edward Cassidy for Maria," Sir Donald said, stripping off his York tan gloves.

"Does the match meet with your approval?" his wife asked.

"Bosh, it's none of my affair, but still George is my relation. Even though he was idiotish enough to entrust Maria to Lavinia's care instead of yours during her come-out, I should hate him to find himself saddled with a son-in-law without a feather to fly with."

"Is Edward so destitute?" she asked, following him into the blue drawing room and accepting a glass of sherry from him.

"Figure of speech, my dear. Like all young beaux, the ready slides through his fingers."

"But just how much has slid?"

Sir Donald sipped his sherry slowly. "That's the question, we'll have to answer. I shouldn't like George's girl to get hitched to a pauper."

"No," Lady Constance agreed, "particularly since she is very nearly one herself."

Although Lady Vyne had not seen anything wrong in keeping the true facts of Maria's fortune from Edward, Maria herself was less certain. She knew Edward to be the dearest, handsomest, most wonderful man in the kingdom, so what difference did her fortune or lack of one make to their relationship?

"Don't be a goose, Maria." Lavinia said tartly. "Edward isn't yours yet, and you would be foolish to spoil matters now when everything is progressing so nicely."

Properly chastened, Maria said nothing more to her aunt but still felt it was wrong to deceive the man she loved. She confided as much to Eleanor later that week when she and Edward accompanied Julia, Eleanor and the ever present Harry Addison on a picnic at Hampton Court.

While Harry led the way, scouting for the best place to spread their blanket, and Julia lagged behind with Edward who was carrying their hamper, Maria had the opportunity to ask her cousin's advice.

"Advice?" Eleanor quizzed, holding the hem of her cornflower-blue walking dress and wondering if Harry were determined to lead them up every hillock on the grounds. "You need no advice from this quarter. You and Edward shall deal splendidly together. Or are you having second thoughts now?"

"I want to tell Edward that Father will be hard-pressed to raise my portion, never mind my being a great heiress, but Aunt Lavinia says I will be a goose-cap if I say a word to him. What do you think I should do?"

"The truth is always commendable," Eleanor said. "I don't think you have anything to fear. Edward is not a fortune hunter. From all I have heard he is very well-pursed himself.''

"Then you think I should tell him the truth?"

"If I were you, I would, but I am not you."

"No," Maria agreed. "It is so vexing. I wish I were you at times. You always know exactly what to do."

"Not always," Eleanor demurred as Harry waved them forward. She still had not come to a decision about Harry. As she climbed, she checked off all of Harry's advantages. He was amiable and kind and handsome. He would cosset her to death—if she didn't die of boredom first.

While Eleanor and Maria hurried up the hillock, Edward and Julia continued to dawdle, engrossed in a discussion concerning the brooch. Julia was determined to have it once again in her possession.

"I don't know, Grimes is a devil," Edward warned, silently speculating on how much money Julia was willing to spend on the brooch.

"He bought it from me for a thousand pounds," Julia reminded him. "And you told me that he wanted fifteen hundred for it now. I have that."

"Yes, I know. But the cutthroat wants an extra thousand. Twenty-five hundred in all."

"But I can't possibly raise that much," she exclaimed in dismay.

"Well, Grimes is firm," Edward said, enjoying his little tête-à-tête. If Julia did hand over twenty-five hundred pounds, he would have some of the debt he owed to Rehagen. "If you doubt my word on this matter you have only to apply to him yourself."

Julia shrank from such a suggestion, exactly as he knew she would.

"I couldn't go near such a horrid place," she said. "I don't think I would have had the courage to go in the first place if I hadn't been in such desperate straits. You will continue to be my emissary, won't you, Mr. Cassidy?"

"As long as you wish, Mrs. Whiting."

"Good. Then I shall just have to find that extra thousand pounds somehow."

Their conversation ended as they reached the hillock where Harry had spread the blanket, and the picnic hamper was quickly opened. Leaving Julia to think over how best to find the extra money she needed, Edward turned his attentions toward Maria. How quickly, he wondered, could he get her to consent to a wedding date? This picnic was his idea but she had insisted on bringing along Julia and Eleanor, and then Addison had appeared and the romantic rendezvous he had envisioned, during which he might determine the exact amount of her fortune, had turned into a family gathering.

Accepting a chicken leg from the basket, Eleanor observed with amusement how eagerly Edward was importuning Maria to put him out of his misery and consent to a quick wedding. Edward was so much in love with her that Maria ought not to delay telling him the truth, Eleanor decided. He wasn't the sort to fly into the boughs over a trifle. In short, he was nothing like Lord Prescott.

She frowned, recalling her aunt's gleeful account of how black Prescott had looked upon learning of Maria's engagement. Had Prescott truly been fixing an interest in Maria? It wasn't his rule to raise groundless expectations in females.

So absorbed was Eleanor in her thoughts that she was roused from her reverie only by Harry's asking her something about Maria's wedding.

"What did you say, Harry?" she asked, brushing some loose blades of grass from her lap.

"I said, what do you think of June for a wedding?"

Had Maria and Eleanor been discussing a June wedding, she wondered guiltily. "Why I think it splendid, of course," she said now.

Harry put down the drumstick he had been gnawing on. "Do you really think so, Eleanor?" he demanded.

"Why, yes," she declared as he wiped his hands meticulously on a napkin before taking her hands in his.

Eleanor felt as though she were in a nightmare when he pulled her toward his bony chest. "Oh, Eleanor, you have made me the happiest man alive!"

THE TRAVEL CHAISE bearing the Prescott family crest stopped in front of the grey stone building. A blonde head peeked out.

"Are we here?" Aimée asked.

"Aye," Walter, the groom replied. "The Convent of the Pious Sisters."

And what would the sisters make of the likes of his employer's ladybird, Walter wondered as he helped her down from the carriage. It wasn't his place to question his lordship's actions, but the groom did think the whole business a trifle havey-cavey.

Aimée stepped briskly onto the stone path and sounded the great knocker on the front door. After a few moments, a white-cowled figure opened the door a crack.

"Yes, Miss?"

"I have come to see a Mademoiselle Rush," Aimée said. "I believe she is staying with you?"

The eyes looked doubtful. "Miss Rush does not wish to see anyone."

"But she must. Please, *ma soeur,* it is very important. I am a friend of hers."

"Your name?"

"Aimée Martine. But she will not know it. Actually, I am a friend of a friend of hers, a man. Not the scoundrel responsible for her condition, but another, a good one, who loves her and wishes to marry her. Please, won't you let me see her."

The nun hesitated, then swung the door open. "Ten minutes, no longer." She led the way into a small sitting room. "I shall fetch her."

Aimée glanced about the bare, unadorned room. A single crucifix on the wall was the only embellishment. She could not help but contrast it to her own lavishly decorated rooms.

"Mademoiselle Martine?" a voice asked.

Aimée glanced up, and saw at once what had smitten young Sebastian. The young woman approaching was tiny, with enormous doelike eyes and soft brown hair. She wore her simple dress with great dignity.

"You are Isabelle," Aimée said. "I am a friend of Sebastian."

"Sebastian." The young woman made an effort to smile. "How is he?"

"I wish I could say he is well."

"Is he ill?"

"Ill for worrying about you."

Isabelle sighed. "He mustn't worry. He must paint."

"He finds that hard to do without you nearby." Aimée patted the couch. "Come, let us sit, *ma petite.* You don't mind my coming here? He would have come himself but he has been turned away. And his letters you do not answer. He was frantic."

"I can't see him. I don't want him to see me like this," Isabelle said, sitting down with Aimée.

"But he wants you still. He wants to marry you. And raise the babe as his own."

"Raise the babe?" Isabelle stared at Aimée. "He can't mean it."

"Would he send me here if he did not mean it?" Aimée demanded. "*Ma petite,* the man is in love with you. He cannot paint half the time for worry over you."

Isabelle gazed down at the wooden floor. "He is too good for me. The babe isn't his."

"That doesn't matter. It will be yours. He will love it. You know Sebastian. Do you doubt that he could do that?"

"No," she said softly, and lifted her eyes. "He is a good man, a wonderful man. I have been a fool, *Mademoiselle.*"

"Everyone is a fool at times," Aimée said. She hugged the girl. "Come now, see how you make an old fool like me cry. Tears of joy, I assure you. Will you come back to London with me?"

"London?"

"*Mais oui.* You will marry Sebastian, and you will have your child with him."

Isabelle pulled away. "I can't go back to London."

"But Sebastian..."

"I will marry Sebastian, but not in London."

A wise smile crossed Aimée's face. "The baby's father lives in London?"

Isabelle nodded.

"He still has power over you? You still love him, desire him?"

"Edward?"

"Is that his name?"

She nodded. "Edward Cassidy. But you must not tell Sebastian. He might challenge him to a duel, and Edward is a crack shot."

"Do you love Edward?"

The young woman emitted a hollow laugh. "No, not anymore."

"Then you must not think any longer about Monsieur Cassidy," Aimée said. "You will come back to London. You will stay with me until we marry you to your Sebastian."

Tears spilled from Isabelle's enormous eyes.

"What is this? Tears?" Aimée clucked. "No, we shall have none of that. You have had enough of tears, I think."

"You are wonderful, Mademoiselle Martine."

Aimée forgot all about the long carriage ride from London.

She kissed the young woman on the forehead. "Now, run along and get your clothes from the sisters," she said, as she sat back on the couch mulling over what to do about a certain Edward Cassidy.

CHAPTER FIFTEEN

"ENGAGED TO HARRY ADDISON? By Jupiter, have you lost your wits?" Sir Donald thundered. The tips of his moustache quivered as his gaze shifted from his daughter to his wife placidly sketching a bowl of fruit. "And you, Madam, have you nothing to say about this coil?"

"If Harry Addison is what Eleanor wants..."

"Of course he's not what I want," Eleanor said, pacing agitatedly across her mother's sitting room.

"You haven't been playing fast and loose with him, have you, Eleanor?"

"Not exactly, Papa."

This reply did not augur well for Sir Donald's state of mind, and he demanded an explanation.

"I did explain," Eleanor said wearily. "We were having a picnic with Julia and Maria. Harry was talking to me and my mind wandered as it often does when I am talking to Harry. When he asked if June would be a suitable month for a wedding, I thought he was talking about Maria and Edward's wedding. So I said, yes. And before I could utter another syllable everyone was wishing me happy."

"Surely you told him it was a mistake," Lady Constance interjected, laying down her charcoal. "How very awkward it will be later for you to cry off."

"I couldn't get a word in. Edward was busy shaking Harry's hand and Maria was kissing me and offering felicitations."

"Hmmph," Sir Donald snorted. "I never did like the notion of picnics. All that fresh air is bound to addle the brain."

"When *do* you plan on telling Harry the truth?" Lady Constance asked.

"Soon," Eleanor said with a sigh.

"You'd best be quick about it," her father said. "When I saw him at White's he was about to pen a letter to his mother telling her all."

Sir Donald quitted the sitting room, leaving Eleanor to ponder the bumblebroth she had created. After several minutes of trying to make a peach look like a peach, Lady Constance laid aside her sketching pad and wiped her hands of the charcoal. She watched her daughter's restless movements about the room.

Eleanor sank down on the couch. "Why is Harry so stupid, Mama? And why wasn't I listening to him today at the picnic? People will call me a horrid flirt after this episode, particularly after what happened earlier with Prescott."

Lady Constance stroked her daughter's dark hair. "Is Prescott still troubling you, Eleanor?"

"No! Prescott would be the worst husband in Christendom."

"If you mean that, Eleanor, you'd do well to forget him completely. You might even take a good look at Harry."

Eleanor could not believe her ears. "Mama, you must be funning. Harry is so agreeable that it would be like arguing with a sponge."

"Would you as liefer have an argumentative spouse?"

Eleanor fell silent, recalling one much too argumentative suitor. "I don't love Harry, Mama," she said.

Lady Constance squeezed her daughter's hand and sighed. "Cupid has done more mischief in the name of love than Mars has in the name of war."

At dinner that evening Sir Donald picked listlessly at his plate, although it contained his usually favoured squab roasted to perfection and covered by a mustard sauce. He paid it scant attention, a sign that his mind was troubled.

"You don't think Eleanor will do something rash about Harry, do you, Constance?" he asked, pushing away his plate at last and putting an end to the pretence of eating. "Only recollect how she ended her engagement to Prescott. You don't think she'll send Harry back some trinket in a bit of muslin?" he asked in the liveliest horror.

"Oh, no! For one thing," she said taking the practical view. "Harry hasn't given her anything to send back. And he's never been that active in the petticoat line. I suspect that she was fonder of Prescott three years ago than she is now of Harry."

"Still, it won't stand to her credit, to break off an engagement again. She'll get the reputation of a flirt."

"Would you rather she enter into a loveless marriage?" his wife asked, slicing a bit of squab and chewing it thoughtfully.

Sir Donald threw down his napkin. "At one time I thought marriage to Prescott would be disastrous. But marrying Harry would be twice as bad. What's the matter with the chit?"

"Nothing that you or I can fix, I fear," Lady Constance said wisely.

ALTHOUGH THE NEWS of Eleanor's acceptance of Harry Addison spread through London, assisted in part by Harry's trumpeting the news at White's, Lord Prescott had not yet learned of the engagement. Unable just to stand idly by and do nothing about Maria Whiting's forthcoming marriage, he had dispatched his secretary to make enquiries about Edward's precise financial standing. The results brought him no peace of mind.

"What exactly is his situation?" Prescott asked Lynch. He sat behind his great mahogany desk and spun his globe absentmindedly.

Mr. Lynch consulted the notes in his hand. "His estates are mortgaged, and his debts considerable. He owes money to all the cent per centers, and has even pawned some of his family jewellery to a moneylender. Nothing there really to signify. A lady's pin, among others, which Grimes said Cassidy had pawned on behalf of Mrs. Julia Whiting. Mrs. Whiting is in debt on account of her gaming."

"Just how scorched is she?"

"Nearly ten thousand pounds."

Prescott pursed his lips. That might account for Julia's irritation on the several occasions when they met. Now that he knew the truth about Edward Cassidy's finances, he wanted to lay the information before someone responsible.

THE NEXT MORNING Prescott ordered his carriage to be brought round for a call on Mount Street.

"Ah, Prescott, I had a nacky notion you might call today," Sir Donald rumbled in greeting. "I've been expecting you. You've had three years to screw your courage to the sticking point."

"Three years?" Prescott asked, looking bewildered.

Sir Donald waved his guest to a seat in the blue drawing room. "I knew that once the word got out, you'd come by. I suspect you needed a few days to collect your thoughts."

"My thoughts on what?" Prescott asked. Sir Donald was not speaking sense.

"About Eleanor, of course."

"What about her?" Prescott asked freezingly.

The smile on Sir Donald's face faded for the first time since the butler had announced Prescott. "Didn't you come here because of her idiotish behaviour with Harry Addison?" he hesitated. "I thought... Well, bless me, I seem to have misjudged the matter. Constance always did say I blundered about. Beg your pardon, Prescott. Enough about that. Why did you wish to see me?"

"About Edward Cassidy. I understand he's offered for Maria. I've learned some important facts about his financial difficulties, which will hardly recommend him as a husband for Maria."

For the next ten minutes Prescott revealed exactly what his secretary had unearthed. He held nothing back, except that he did not mention that Edward had acted on behalf of Julia Whiting. Sir Donald's benevolent face darkened during parts of the recital.

"If this is true—"

"I am not in the habit of lying," Prescott said languidly.

"I'm not saying you are," Sir Donald replied, beetling his brow. "But I'll put my own man onto it just the same, Prescott. He'll confirm your facts if they are facts. Until then I'll keep Maria and Edward from dashing to the altar."

"Good." Prescott breathed a sigh of relief. "I don't like to think of such an innocent in the hands of a scoundrel like him."

Sir Donald offered his guest a glass of Madeira, but Lord Prescott declined. He had accomplished what he had set out to do. It was only when he was nearing Manton's that he realized he hadn't thought to enquire just what idiotish thing Eleanor had done with Harry.

He found out soon enough from Philip Hawthorne whom he met on his way into the shooting gallery.

"Engaged to Harry Addison!" Prescott turned nearly as rigid as his collar points. "What game is she running now!"

"I don't know if it is a game. Diana thinks Eleanor just felt sorry for Harry. He's been dangling after her for three months."

"Three months is nothing. He should try three years," Prescott murmured as they entered the target room.

"What's that you say?"

"Nothing, just talking to myself."

Philip shot first, scoring a bull's-eye and appearing disconcerted that his friend, usually a crack shot, could not find the target that day.

"Diana thought you might be offering for Eleanor soon." He ventured.

Prescott's mouth set in a grim line. "Did that once before." He pulled the trigger.

"Missed again," Philip observed. "You don't hold that against Eleanor, do you? The breach appeared to be on the mend."

Prescott gave a hollow laugh. "Eleanor still holds me in considerable dislike. Perhaps on account of her cousin, Maria." He rued the day he had decided to pretend to be interested in Maria in order to pique Eleanor's own interest. "Now would you stop chattering while I try to shoot?"

Agreeably, Mr. Hawthorne fell silent, which left Lord Prescott to his shooting and his thoughts. He wasn't such a dolt as to offer for Eleanor again when she made it plain she would not entertain his suit. He knew he loved her and that she was the only lady he would wed. But a man could only endure so much rejection.

Still, that didn't mean she ought to marry a gudgeon like Harry Addison. Unfortunately he could not point this out to her. But perhaps if he dropped a word in someone's ear. Andrew would have been ideal, but since he was still at Oakmore, maybe his wife would be of some assistance.

Since Philip had mentioned that Eleanor would be accompanying Diana on another sitting for her portrait later than afternoon, Prescott lost no time in paying a call at Cavendish Square.

"Lord Prescott!" Julia appeared stunned at the sight of her caller.

"Do forgive my bursting in on you this way, Mrs. Whiting," he said in his friendliest tone, "but it was the only time that would serve. Philip Hawthorne told me that Eleanor would be accompanying his wife on an errand, and I simply must see you and talk to you."

"Lord Prescott, I must warn you that if you lay one hand on me I shall scream! And not in ecstasy, I assure you!" Julia added defiantly.

"Ecstasy? I assure you, Mrs. Whiting..."

"I know your intentions with females, and while some may enjoy acting in a reckless fashion, I do not! That is why I must tell you again that your attempts to make love to me are unwelcome."

"Attempts to make what?" he asked incredulously.

"Make love," she said, watching as he sank down onto the couch.

"Mrs. Whiting, I know my abominable memory, but I have no recollection of ever, as you put it, attempting to make love to you."

"You don't recall coming to see me on the matter of my debt to Lord Foxworth and telling me that something could be arranged of mutual benefit?"

Prescott stared at her. "And from that you deduced... Good heavens!" The shock on his face was sincere enough to give Julia a moment's pause. "I am not such a scoundrel, I assure you. I meant only that you could pay it off in your own time and your own way. Did you tell your husband of your suspicions?"

"No."

"Thank God for that."

His evident sincerity soon convinced Julia she had mistaken the matter. "But if you didn't come bent on seduction, why are you here now?"

"Eleanor. She can't be allowed to marry Harry Addison," he said. "Unfortunately, she's not disposed to listen to anything I say, so I thought perhaps I could appeal to you. Could you not use your considerable influence to dissuade her from such a fatal step?''

"You love her, don't you?''

"Mrs. Whiting!''

Julia smiled, noticing the varying emotions on Prescott's face. "I think you ought to speak to her yourself.''

"I would, if she would sit and listen to me.''

"Tonight we go to Vauxhall Gardens to see the fireworks. If you arrange to be there as well, I shall try to give you a few moments alone with her.''

"Mrs. Whiting, if you do that, I shall be forever in your debt.''

She gave a rueful laugh as she held out her hand for him to kiss. "In my debt? That is rich, particularly since I am in practically everyone else's debt at the moment!''

"May I be of some assistance there?''

"Oh, no. My luck will turn. As it is, I have practically enough to pay off my most pressing debts. Or at least I would if Aunt Lavinia weren't so insistent on seeing that dreadful pin.''

"Pin?'' he asked, looking bewildered.

Julia realized her slip. "It's an heirloom that Mr. Cassidy was kind enough to help me sell.''

"To a moneylender?''

She coloured. "Yes, his name is Grimes. The ruby pin is the most hideous thing imaginable. But Aunt Lavinia wishes to see it and order one for herself. I've managed to fob her off and I have nearly enough to redeem it.''

"Say no more,'' Prescott said, taking out his purse.

"Lord Prescott!''

"Your situation is causing you pain...''

"But I can't. I won't let you pay for my folly. No. I shall just trust to Lady Luck to be good to me."

Seeing the adamant look on her face, he did not insist, but merely took his leave of her. However instead of turning in at Berkeley Square, his phaeton continued across the Strand toward the City, in whose darker regions his secretary had assured him he could find a certain Mr. Grimes.

CHAPTER SIXTEEN

JULIA FOUND temporary respite from her vexing financial travails in Eleanor's romantic one. Nothing, she vowed to herself, could be more romantic than Prescott's tendre for Eleanor which had endured three years of silence.

"Why do you bring his name up?" Eleanor asked, on her return to Cavendish Square. Being obliged to sit for one's portrait was fatiguing, but being obliged to wait while one's companion was painted was equally tiresome.

"I speak of Lord Prescott because he came calling today," Julia replied.

"Did he attempt to make love to you?"

"No, no, I mistook the matter, Eleanor. He didn't have any interest in me at all. He is interested in you."

"That gentleman changes his fancy quicker than the weather," Eleanor said with an audible sniff, although her heart lurched at Julia's last words.

"I don't think it's a change," Julia said. "He seemed quite in earnest. He has been wearing the willow for three years."

Eleanor turned away, displeasure writ large on her face. Prescott had dispatched his mistress to the country, and now he sought to resume his courtship. No doubt he thought he had only to lift a finger and Eleanor would snatch him up.

"Lord Prescott is a scoundrel and a rake. And if he did try to speak to me I would wish him to Jericho. Do you really wish to go to Vauxhall Gardens this evening?" Eleanor asked, changing the subject.

"Oh yes, we must go. I heard it will be quite the best exhibition there ever was. And don't you remember asking Harry to join us?"

"Yes," Eleanor turned pensive. Perhaps Harry was the reason for the deplorable lack of anticipation she felt for the evening ahead. "I fear I must tell him that our match cannot be, and yet I dislike hurting him."

"A brief rest will put you to rights," Julia suggested. "Do go abovestairs and nap. I can send Millie with some lilac water, if you wish. Undoubtedly, you have a good deal on your mind, feeling the way you do about Harry and Prescott."

Now what did Julia mean by that, Eleanor wondered as she lay down in her bed chamber. Harry was the most agreeable fellow in the ton, handsome, too, and bound to be a doting husband. And Prescott? His rakish disposition would bring any wife to misery. Eleanor was glad that she herself had put her feeling for him behind her.

"Are you sure about that?" An inward voice sceptically questioned her.

"Yes, I have," she replied defiantly. "I have put Prescott behind me."

She turned over on her side. How complicated life was! It was far more bearable when she and Prescott were in each other's black books. Then she knew what to do: turn him the cold shoulder. Now she felt unsure and vulnerable. How she wished Andrew was home. Then she could leave Cavendish Square and return to Mount Street, and everything would be back to normal. Or would it?

Eleanor sat up, out of patience with this missish vacillating. Tonight at the exhibition she would tell Harry that she couldn't marry him. No doubt he would take it badly, but she could not delay it any longer.

And yet when Harry called for her that evening, looking quite handsome in his swallow-tailed coat and expertly knotted cravat she was obliged to admit that he did look very dashing.

Since the night was cloudless and ideal for fireworks, the Gardens were crowded. As they joined the throng making their way toward the observation area, Eleanor noticed Edward and Maria.

Maria might be a featherhead, but she had determined this once that she would not lie to her Edward any more. She would tell him the truth about her supposed fortune. No doubt they would have a good laugh over the strategem Lady Vyne had chosen to adopt. And yet, she hesitated to broach the subject immediately. Thus she eagerly joined Eleanor's group.

"The fireworks will start shortly," Edward said.

"We can get a good view from over there," Eleanor said and they all moved dutifully toward the left. Julia had been keeping an eye out for Lord Prescott, and she now recognized his tall, aristocratic figure. She dropped behind the others in her group and motioned him to join her.

"Lord Prescott, you must not speak to Eleanor," she informed him.

Prescott frowned, rather put out by first being told to present himself at Vauxhall Gardens for the tête-à-tête with Eleanor and now being informed that he must not speak.

"Mrs. Whiting, you yourself told me today—"

"But Eleanor is still very resolved against you. If you approach her now, she may only wish you to Jericho. You cannot desire a public display of her displeasure."

"No," he agreed, grimacing at the idea. "But what do you recommend, for I do wish to speak to her."

"After the fireworks, I shall contrive to send her over there," Julia said, indicating one of the walkways. "If you happen to see her alone, you can then make your declaration as you see fit."

Prescott nodded. "A very good scheme. Thank you, Mrs. Whiting. I am grateful."

"You haven't won her yet," Julia reminded him. "And I must warn you she is very set against you. I can't think why, unless it's because of what I told her about your attempts to seduce me," she said, feeling a pang of guilt.

"Eleanor has ample reason to feel the way she does, but it will be my place to change her mind once and for all," he said, disappearing back into the crowd.

"Julia, where have you been?" Eleanor exclaimed when Julia wove her way back toward the steps. "We feared you might have been trampled."

"No, I was just feeling a trifle faint and stopped to take the air."

"Then stand over here." Eleanor switched places immediately. "The fireworks are about to start."

No sooner had she spoken than a resounding boom could be heard and the sky was pierced by a display of red and blue lights in the shape of a flower.

"Ohh..." Maria exclaimed at this, her first fireworks display.

Edward tightened his arm about her. "Don't be frightened."

"Oh, I'm not. It's too thrilling!"

While Eleanor, too, enjoyed the display she found something sad about the lights exploding so giddily in the sky, hovering there for an incandescent moment and then drifting away to nothing. Like love, the beauty simply didn't last.

After twenty minutes the fireworks were over, and the crowd started to disperse. Julia waited for the right moment and saw her opportunity when Harry and Eleanor were temporarily separated by Mrs. Drummond Burrell who swept through with the regal dignity befitting a Patroness.

"Good heavens, did you see her?" Eleanor declared to Julia, catching her to keep her balance. "If she weren't a Patroness..."

"But she is," Julia reminded her.

"Oh heavens, now we've lost Harry." Eleanor glanced first one way and then the other in the thick of the crowd. "We'll be here till dawn trying to find him."

"We'll search for him," Julia said, "you go that way." She pointed Eleanor down to the pathway she had indicated to Lord Prescott. "We'll meet here later. Agreed?"

"All right," Eleanor said, amazed at the purposefulness her sister-in-law was displaying of late.

As Eleanor strolled off, Julia's keen eye spotted Harry in the distance. Quickly she intercepted him.

"Mrs. Whiting? But where is Eleanor?" he asked, glancing about.

"I believe she went down that path, Harry, looking for you," Julia said, indicating a path opposite the one Eleanor had taken. "Would you be so kind as to follow it? I shall remain here in case she comes back."

Along that same path which Harry was following, Edward and Maria were now strolling. Edward was pressing Maria to set the date for the wedding, and she was trying to find the right words to tell him about her lack of fortune. Face-to-face with him in the moonlight, she found her courage waning.

"Maria, what is amiss?" Edward entreated.

"Nothing whatever, Edward."

"You have not rethought the matter? Changed your mind?" he asked, his indulgent tone hiding his real anxiety. She must not change her mind about marrying him.

"No, of course not," she said hastily.

"Good." He bent down and stroked her hair lightly. She was comely enough and he would undoubtedly enjoy bedding her. Thinking of that, he bent and kissed her long and deeply. Maria, a bit taken aback by such a kiss in so deserted an area, broke free almost at once. True, they were engaged, but . . .

"Edward!"

"You mustn't scold me. I am under your spell." He kissed her again, harder this time.

"Edward, please," Maria exclaimed, frightened by his actions.

"You will get accustomed to a man's kisses," Edward said, huskily.

"No, please!" Maria said, relieved when she heard footsteps coming down the path. Harry Addison peered at them in the moonlight.

"Oh, I beg pardon, Edward, Miss Whiting. Have either of you seen Eleanor?"

"No," Edward said.

"I think I saw her earlier," Maria spoke up.

Harry's face brightened. "Oh, could you tell me where?"

"I'll show you," Maria said, taking his arm.

"Oh, that's deuced civil of you. Didn't mean to interrupt," Harry chattered on amiably, and in his company Maria was able to recover her countenance.

ON THE OTHER PATH Eleanor was beginning to wonder where Harry had gone. The path was darker than she would have liked, and she wished that Julia had come with her.

Just when she thought she would never find him, she saw a figure in a black swallow-tailed coat looming up before her.

"Harry!" she cried out with relief.

Prescott turned, the happy tone in her voice uttering Addison's name stabbing him to the quick.

"Oh, it's you," she said, recognizing him. There could be no mistaking the change in her voice. "I thought it was Harry."

"So I deduce," Prescott said, managing to keep a civil tongue as he stepped closer. The moonlight danced in her hair, and her eyes glowed. She looked more beautiful than ever. How had he ever let her get away?

His scrutiny made her flush. "You must excuse me, Lord Prescott. I must find Harry."

Her words broke his reverie, and he caught her by the wrist as she moved to pass. "I must speak to you, Miss Whiting. A moment of your time is all I ask."

"Let me go!" she exclaimed. "I don't wish to speak to you."

"Then just listen," he said, pulling her close in a viselike embrace. "I love you. You cannot marry Addison, do you hear me. You must marry me."

Her reaction surprised him. She beat her fists on his chest, laughing and yet sobbing at the same time.

"Odious, odious man! How dare you! Do you think I am no better than a trollop? Love me? You cannot love anyone. Even your mistress Aimée knows that by now. You are too vain, selfish, self-serving."

He caught her fists in his hands and kissed them. "If you are still troubled by Aimée, you needn't be. She means nothing to me. It's over between us. It's you I love, Eleanor. I've always loved you."

Eleanor's lip curled, aghast that he would throw Aimée aside now that she was with child and play the part of a lovesick swain to her.

"I beg you let go of me, sir," she said coldly. "I find this entire spectacle revolting."

"Revolting!" Prescott's temper flared. He had humbled himself in front of her and this is the way she treated him. "Very well. You'll hear not another word from me."

He flung down her wrist and turned away, then just as abruptly he turned back to her and snatched her up again, crushing his lips down on hers.

Taken by surprise, Eleanor had hardly time to think, let alone fight him off, and one part of her, the treacherous side, did not want to fight him off. His kiss was all that she remembered, intoxicating, breathtaking, a promise of what could be. She met his passion with hers, her mouth searching his for a response that her mind said was foolish.

"You love me," he exclaimed, as she finally wrenched away from him.

"No!" she exclaimed. "I don't love you. I can't love you. I won't love you."

He looked down into her eyes, aware of the tumultuous pounding of her heart beneath her warm breasts.

"Does Harry Addison kiss you that way?" he asked softly. "More to the point, do you kiss Harry that way? I love you. I have made mistakes, more than a few, but that is the past. Marry me."

She stared at him, stricken for a moment by the betrayal of her own heart. What a ninnyhammer she was! It was stupid to love him so, knowing what she did of him.

"I can't," she said, and fled up the path.

Julia, who was lying in wait, saw immediately that the rendezvous had not gone as she had hoped.

"Eleanor?"

"Oh, Julia," she said as she fell into her sister-in-law's arms. "Please find Harry and take me home."

CHAPTER SEVENTEEN

ELEANOR TOSSED AND TURNED on her bed, her mind at sixes and sevens. A few mistakes indeed! He had cast off Aimée and the babe she awaited, and now expected Eleanor to snatch him up. Well, he was wrong!

And yet the memory of his kisses burned in her flesh. She could not erase them, and by morning she was exhausted. Andrew's return proved a welcome diversion.

"You've had enough of rural tranquillity?" Eleanor quizzed him at lunch after her brother had bathed and exchanged his travel-stained apparel for his usual elegant morning dress.

Andrew smiled. "More than enough," he said emphatically. "I thought Prescott was joking about the state of neglect, but Oakmore is in dire straits indeed."

"Do you still mean to purchase it?" Julia asked, taking a sip of her turtle soup.

"No, my love. I shall have to tell Prescott so later. I do hope Mrs. Edgewater isn't too dashed down by my decision."

"She may be relieved. She is very attached to the estate," Eleanor said.

No more was said about the Edgewater estate as the three applied themselves assiduously to the roasted partridges, turtle soup, and other delicacies from the kitchen.

"And what have you two been up to in my absence?" Andrew asked, accepting a dish of strawberries and cream.

"The biggest news afoot is Maria's acceptance of Mr. Edward Cassidy." His wife told him.

"Really? Quite a feather in Edward's cap to win her over all the other sprigs. Wasn't Prescott dangling after her?"

"Do tell us more about your trip, Andrew," Julia spoke quickly, seeing the shadow come over Eleanor's eyes again.

"There isn't much to tell," Andrew said. "I spent most of my days looking over the estate. The servants were glad of the company. They are incurable gossips, I suppose you know. At one point they swore that Prescott was on his way to the estate, too."

"Prescott? But he's been in London for a fortnight."

"Yes, I know. It was only his travel chaise they had seen in the vicinity. I had an embarrassing moment on account of it," he confessed.

"Oh?"

"When I saw the chaise I assumed Prescott was within, so I knocked on the door. And..." For the first time Andrew hesitated.

"And?" his sister prompted.

"Well, it wasn't him, Eleanor. It was that friend of his. Aimée Martine. I apologized for interrupting her and left, but it was a bit of an embarrassment."

"What would Prescott's chère amie be doing in Wiltshire?" Julia asked.

Eleanor could have enlightened her, but she kept silent. Andrew's encounter with Aimée merely confirmed what she already knew. Aimée had been dispatched to the country until she had Prescott's baby.

AT THAT VERY MOMENT Aimée was trying to get Isabelle to climb the stairs to Sebastian's atelier. During the trip back to London the girl's courage had deserted her, and she would have bolted if not for the hand Aimée kept clamped to her wrist.

"You say you love him, what is the matter?" the Frenchwoman asked, losing patience.

"He can't love me...I should never have left the convent."

"Bah!" Aimée had had enough of such missishness. She knocked once on the door, then again.

"See, he's not here!"

The door opened and Sebastian, palette in hand, stood frowning at them. "What do you—Aimée! Isabelle? Is she here?"

"*Voilà,*" Aimée said, pushing the girl forward.

"Oh, Isabelle!" Sebastian exclaimed, throwing his arms around her. Aimée prudently removed the palette from his grasp as he got down to the serious business of kissing his beloved.

The sight of the two young lovers entwined in each other's arms brought tears to Aimée's own eyes. *I am getting to be a romantic old fool,* she thought.

"Mademoiselle Aimée, how can we ever thank you," Sebastian said.

"Love each other, be happy," Aimée said, hunting in her reticule for her handkerchief.

"We shall, we shall. And we shall be married at once. Come, let's find a church!"

Aimée dabbed her eyes with the handkerchief while Isabelle implored Sebastian to be sensible.

"Don't be so anxious, my dear ones. You can procure a special licence and be married tomorrow," Aimée advised.

"I suppose I can wait one day," Sebastian said, looking impatient.

A few minutes later, alone, and feeling all the satisfaction of a job well done, Aimée descended the stairs. Those two would do well together. Sebastian would paint his pictures, and Isabelle would be his devoted wife and model.

She sank back into the Prescott chaise. Seeing Sebastian with Isabelle had sparked a longing in her heart for Armand, and she gave the order to the groom to pull in at his lodgings. She half expected to find him still asleep, but he was in his studio, arranging his canvases.

"Aimée!" He swept her up in his arms, oblivious to the paint on his face and hands.

"Armand! What is this? Up before noon?"

He kissed her soundly and then released her. "Aimée, will you marry me?" he asked seriously.

Aimée, a bit dizzy from being kissed, and then thrust aside, held up her hands at this familiar question.

"You love me, I know."

"We have been over this before. I love you, but marriage—" she shrugged "—it is quite a different thing from love."

"You and I know just how different," Armand said. He was grinning at her. "Is it the money that worries you?"

"*Zut!* You make me sound like a fortune hunter," she protested.

He caught her hands in his and kissed them. "I have money. In fact, I have something better than money."

"What is better than money?" she asked naively.

"A patron!"

She stared at him as he did a little jig about his crowded studio. "Patron?" she asked.

"Yes. After you left, I received a call from Honoré DuChamp. You recall him, I hope?"

"The very fat one with the Paris gallery."

"Yes, he's even fatter now, and his Paris gallery is even larger. He was interested in my work. When I asked why, he finally confessed that someone wanted to sponsor an exhibit for me. And what is more, my patron will give me a thousand pounds a month, plus what my paintings bring in."

A thousand pounds a month was a very good income, more than some gentlemen she knew had at their disposal.

"Now, will you marry me?" he asked.

Aimée blinked back tears. "Yes," she said. "I shall marry you." She reached out her arms for him and instantly he was in them.

"And the best part is we must live in Paris," he said a little later. "It is one of the conditions of my patron."

Paris. Aimée sighed. To see Paris again. To be home again. It was a dream come true.

"But do you know who your patron is, Armand?"

"Some lover of the arts. Perhaps, it could even be the Regent."

"The Regent?"

"He is a generous man. The identity does not concern me too greatly."

It did, however, concern Aimée.

"A PATRON OF SAINT JACQUES? What a quaint notion, my dear Aimée," Prescott drawled an hour later in his blue drawing room. Aimée had returned his chaise and had agreed to a glass of sherry.

"Don't dissemble, Prescott. You are the only one who would do such a thing."

"And why would I?" he demanded.

Her eyes met his and softened. "Perhaps because you would like to be rid of me," she teased.

"Never," he said gallantly. "It is you who have replaced me with Armand in your heart."

"Prettily said," Aimée observed. "Very well. I shall pretend I don't know you are the one responsible for Armand's good fortune. His paintings are good and will be valuable some day."

"I'm sure they will be." He handed her a glass of sherry. "Are you marrying him, then?"

"Yes, we will be going to Paris to live."

He held up his glass. "Then, to Paris."

"To Paris," she agreed, drinking deeply.

"How did your little mission of mercy go?"

"It went very well. Those two are also going to be married. So all's well that ends well, as you English say. Except that I would wish a certain person by the name of Edward Cassidy to be hanged by the neck till he is dead."

Prescott lifted a craggy brow. "Harsh words, Aimée."

"He deserves them. Seducing little Isabelle and then throwing her aside. No gentleman would act like that."

"You're sure it was Edward's doing?"

"Isabelle told me so herself. Not that I can do very much about it. She swore me to secrecy. The sherry has loosened my tongue."

"I promise not to divulge it," he reassured her immediately. "Edward's day of reckoning is fast approaching. Maria Whiting had accepted him but I spoke with Sir Donald yesterday. I believe he will scotch the match."

"Good," Aimée said with a sigh. She took another companionable sip of her sherry and glanced over at Prescott. "All this talk of love and intrigue, Prescott. It's too fatiguing."

"I quite agree," he said. He smiled, but she noticed the dark circles around his eyes.

"What is amiss?"

"Nothing that seeing you does not fix."

She waved away his flattery. "What has *she* done?"

"She?"

Aimée placed her glass on the tray. "Miss Whiting. Eleanor. It must be she, for only one female I know could make you change your mood so."

For a moment Prescott toyed with the idea of denying it. Then he shrugged.

"You know me too well, Aimée. And as for Eleanor, why she's done nothing at all, except turn down my offer once again."

"*Chéri,* you must go to her and sweep her up in your arms and tell her you love her. She will not be able to resist that."

He laughed. "I did all that, Aimée, and to no avail."

"She refused your kisses?"

"No." A sober look came into his eyes. "She didn't refuse them, but she doesn't want me," he said in a tone that struck Aimée to the core. He raked his fingers through his hair. "It's too late, Aimée. I should have gone to her earlier. I let three years slip by, and I cannot recapture her."

Aimée squeezed his hand. "My dear friend, you will. Just go to her again."

"No!" he said, his face so fierce she was a little frightened. "I humbled myself once in front of her. I won't do it again. I am going to do what I should have done three years ago. I am going to forget her or die trying."

"MR. REHAGEN'S COMPLIMENTS, Mr. Cassidy."

Edward gasped as a large fist bounced off his stomach.

"Just a little reminder about the money you owe."

"I need no reminder," Edward protested, before another fist could descend. "He shall get his money."

"Good." A large hand picked him up from his parlour floor. "Three thousand pounds."

"Three! I owe him but two."

"Interest, for making him wait," the large man said. He set the large beaver felt back on Edward's head. "Good day to your worship," he bowed and sauntered off, laughing loudly.

An hour later Edward pulled his carriage to a stop at Lord Vyne's establishment and within a few minutes was persuading Maria to come with him on a drive in the Park. Lady Vyne proved a welcome ally in this mission.

"Yes, do go on with Edward, my love."

"But, Aunt, what about our call on Julia and Andrew? You wanted to see that brooch."

"I shall go alone. They will understand. Run along and change, my dear. You don't wish to keep Mr. Cassidy waiting."

Alone with Lady Vyne, Edward chatted comfortably about the parties during the week, deploring with her the fact that Prinny was squandering such huge sums on that Pavilion in Brighton.

Privately his thoughts dwelt not on Prinny but on Maria. With each day that passed his situation grew more desperate. Rehagen was not a man to keep waiting. Edward had been anxiously anticipating word about his uncle's death. He could not risk sending another bottle of poisoned tonic to him. His only other recourse was Maria and her fortune.

"Such a nice, agreeable girl, don't you agree?" Lady Vyne turned an enquiring eye toward her guest.

"Indeed." He smiled his most winning smile at her. "I grow impatient at the delays for our wedding."

"Spoken like Romeo himself, Mr. Cassidy," Lady Vyne said. "Ah, here is Maria, and not a moment too soon, I daresay."

Looking quite fetching in a lemon-yellow day dress and matching chip hat, Maria ascended easily into Edward's vehicle.

"Where are we going?" she asked.

"Just for a ride in the Park," he said. She had seemed skittish of late, not even giving him time alone with her. Either Julia was underfoot, or Eleanor, or sometimes even that bore Harry Addison. But today he had a clear path, and he meant to press his suit.

"You know I love you, Maria," he said, pulling his carriage to a stop at the Serpentine. "Why do you delay? I can have a special licence drawn. We can be married tomorrow!"

"What? Oh Edward, you are jesting."

"Your family approves of me. Your aunt is for our marriage."

"Yes, I know. But Uncle Donald told me to wait until my father wrote his approval."

Edward gnashed his teeth. There was one way to make certain she would marry him. And yet, in broad daylight?

"Besides, I think there is something you should know about me."

"I know everything that matters," he said indulgently. He had gathered from Lady Vyne that her fortune came to at least twenty thousand pounds.

"No, you don't. I told Aunt Lavinia that I wanted to tell you the truth. I never did lie to you, Edward. It was she who put the story about. Not that I blame her, for she was just trying to help me."

"What are you talking about?" he asked brusquely.

"My fortune."

She had his complete attention now. "What about it?" he demanded.

Her lips trembled. He looked even more fierce than before.

"I don't have any," she said, taking her fences in a rush.

"You don't have any fortune?" he said, each word spoken slowly. "What are you saying? You have a fortune of at least twenty thousand."

"No, no, I don't!" she exclaimed. "Papa will be hard-pressed to even raise my portion . . ."

"What!" Edward grabbed her by the shoulders and shook her. "Are you trying to trick me, you stupid chit?"

"No! Ohh . . . you're hurting me!"

"What are you doing to Miss Whiting?" a voice demanded.

Edward dropped his hands and glanced over his shoulder. Harry Addison had pulled up, his usually benevolent face dark with anger. He and Eleanor stepped down from their vehicle.

"Nothing that concerns you."

"We'll see about that," Eleanor began, but Harry had already extended a hand to Maria.

"If Miss Whiting is in danger, it concerns me greatly," Harry said. "Do step down from there, Miss Whiting," he said soothingly. "I shall be happy to escort you home."

Eleanor was dumbfounded at this metamorphosis in her companion.

"Oh, thank you, Mr. Addison, and Eleanor."

"Take her, then," Edward snorted. "Silly-headed chit. She doesn't have a fortune. Do you know that?" he sneered and drove away.

"You told him, then?" Eleanor asked, correctly surmising the reason for the contretemps.

"Yes. He was terrible. A monster. I was never so frightened." She looked up at Harry. "Thank you so much, Mr. Addison."

"I did only what any gentleman would have done," Harry said, nonetheless feeling a certain satisfaction at the admiring face held up toward him.

CHAPTER EIGHTEEN

FORGETTING ELEANOR was not as simple a task as Lord Prescott had imagined. An hour after Aimée departed, Andrew Whiting called, announcing his decision not to purchase Oakmore.

"Hope you'll understand, Prescott. The repair to the first floor alone will be considerable."

"I fully understand your reasons," Prescott said, and the two men parted on good terms.

Hoping for a few hours' peace, Prescott went off to White's where he glimpsed Sir Donald behind the *Racing News* in the reading room. Were all of Eleanor's relations destined to haunt him, he wondered. As if in answer to that question he found Lady Constance in the green drawing room when he called on Mrs. Edgewater to relay word of Andrew's decision.

"Well, Peter, come in. You know Lady Constance of course," his aunt said briskly.

"Of course. How do you do, ma'am?" Prescott bowed.

"Very well," Lady Constance said, smiling at him.

"Sit down, Peter, and take this cup of tea. It's a new blend from the Berry Brothers. Chinese. We are discussing my ball next week. It will be a small affair but you must attend."

His lordship sipped his tea, attempting to find a way of excusing himself from the ball. His aunt would undoubtedly invite Eleanor.

"What night is it?" he enquired, putting down the Dresden china cup.

"Friday."

"I'm sorry, Aunt Judith," he said, hoping his tone sounded regretful, "but on Friday I am promised to the Opera."

"Then we shall make it Saturday," Mrs. Edgewater said with aplomb. "I won't accept any excuses, Peter. If it's too dreary you can always escape to the card room."

He gave in with good grace.

"And now, what brings you by?" Mrs. Edgewater asked, "unless it's to see how much further I am in decrepitude."

"You are no such thing and well you know it!" Prescott said. "Even now I could count five gentlemen waiting for you to say the word so they may make a declaration."

Mrs. Edgewater emitted a crackle of laughter.

"Actually, Aunt Judith, I've come because Andrew Whiting has decided against purchase of the estate."

Mrs. Edgewater accepted this news with equanimity. "Yes, I know. Andrew doesn't lack for manners, and he called on me earlier. I have decided that since it will cost too much to refurbish properly, and no one of any sense will buy it, that I shall offer the property to the Church."

"The Church?" Prescott ejaculated at the same time as Lady Constance.

"Don't you think that an excellent scheme?" Their hostess enquired, glancing from face to face. "*They* have the money and the power to refurbish it."

"I'm sure they do," Lady Constance said, "but what would they do with the estate?"

"Who knows?" Mrs. Edgewater was suddenly convulsed with giggles and choked on a laugh.

"Judith!" Lady Constance bent over her with a glass of water.

"I'm fine. I was just trying to imagine the Squire's expression if he knew that nuns or monks would be inhabiting his favourite stomping grounds."

Prescott's lips twitched as well.

"I know Aldridge will dislike the scheme," Mrs. Edgewater said. "So would you speak to him about it, Peter? My head is too full with plans for my ball."

"Very well, Aunt Judith," he said.

"And mind, I'll hold you to your promise to appear at eight sharp Saturday night."

"Eight, it is," he promised, finally able to take his leave.

After a comfortable cose with Mrs. Edgewater, on the topic of her daughter and her hostess's nephew, Lady Constance returned to Mount Street where she found her establishment in an uproar.

Her drawing room was inhabited by a weeping Maria, a livid Lavinia and a rather bemused Eleanor, who was assiduously applying a vinaigrette alternately to Maria and to Lavinia.

"What has happened?" Lady Constance demanded.

To this simple question three voices attempted answers. But it was Harry Addison who finally furnished the explanation.

"Edward Cassidy is nought but a fortune hunter!"

"Ah."

"Silly chit." Lady Vyne focussed her wrath on the weeping Maria, "spoiling the excellent match I had arranged."

"I hardly think marriage to a fortune hunter qualifies as excellent," Harry said, surprising both Constance and Lavinia.

"This is a family matter, Mr. Addison," Lady Vyne said in her top-loftiest manner. "I'll thank you to stay out of it."

"Harry is right," Lady Constance said, paying no attention to Lavinia's strictures. "I congratulate Maria on telling the truth."

"Easy for you to say! You only have the one daughter to marry off," Lady Vyne exclaimed. "I'm sure George will have a different opinion. And I just wrote to him yesterday that Maria had made an excellent match here."

The arrival of Sir Donald sparked a fresh outbreak of tears from Maria and the threat of vapours from Lady Vyne.

"Enough, enough!" Sir Donald expostulated. "I can hardly think straight. Addison?"

"Yes?" Harry jerked his head up in surprise.

"I'd be obliged if you would escort Maria home."

"Why yes, of course," Harry said agreeably.

"But Donald!" Lavinia protested.

"Do it now, Addison." Sir Donald commanded. As soon as the pair had gone off, he turned to his sister. "Now, Lavinia, what, pray, is all this?"

"The match has gone awry because of Maria's stupidity."

"Edward Cassidy is a fortune hunter," Lady Constance interjected.

"Yes, I know," her husband replied.

"You know, Papa!" Eleanor raised a brow. "This is the first I've heard of it."

"It won't be the last," Sir Donald drawled. "He's kept it a secret, thanks to some generous moneylenders, but it's goose to guineas that the truth will out soon, particularly since he owes a goodly sum to a villain by the name of Rehagen. That's probably why he pressed Maria for an early wedding. With the fortune he thought she possessed he could pay off Rehagen and some of his other debts."

"Why did you suspect Edward?" Eleanor asked. "I never did."

For a moment Sir Donald thought of crediting Prescott with the suspicions, but remembering the unpleasantness between his daughter and that gentleman, he decided the less he mentioned Prescott the better.

"I am not a complete fool," Sir Donald said.

"No, but I am," Lavinia said slowly. "George will be livid once he hears what has happened. I was to look after Maria."

"He won't be too annoyed. I have already written and given him the bad news about Edward. I told him you didn't know and so he ought to contrive an excuse for not wishing an early wedding. And as for Maria herself, once she has finished feeling sorry for herself, she will be happy to be rid of Edward."

"And then we will be back to where we started, with finding her a husband. And the Season is nearly completed!" Lady Vyne wailed.

"Maria is a sweet child. She may surprise you by taking one of her other admirers. She has quite a few dangling after her, you must recall."

"So she does," Lady Vyne said, an altered expression on her face.

Suitors like Lord Prescott, Eleanor thought gloomily, as she climbed the stairs. But even though she had been wrong about Edward, she knew that she was not wrong about Prescott. And she would do everything in her power to prevent Maria's falling victim to him.

SINCE MR. ALDRIDGE was still away in Northumbria, Lord Prescott was not able to tell him about his aunt's wish to donate her country estate to charity. He left word at Aldridge's office that he had called and on Thursday morning was pleasantly surprised to find Aldridge waiting for him.

"Aldridge, there was no need to come calling on me here," he said.

"I do beg your pardon, my lord, but I have been wanting to see you. When I read your note about Oakmore I came right over."

"I know you wish to talk her out of it, and I beg you do not. She has hit upon the perfect solution. No one else wants the house and the estate with the cost of repairs. So let the Church have it with our blessing."

"Oh, that, yes." The solicitor bobbed his head. "A bit out of the ordinary, but I think it a novel solution to her dilemma. But it was not on that matter that I wished to speak to you, sir. Do you recall my telling you about my visit to Lord Fenley?"

Prescott nodded, his expression polite but baffled.

Aldridge pulled a bottle from his pocket. "Do you know what this is, sir?"

"Appears to be a medicine," Prescott said, wrinkling his nose involuntarily.

"That's right. It comes from Fenley."

"Did you have a touch of the grippe, then?" Prescott asked solicitously.

"Yes, and Fenley offered me a tonic. He'd just opened a new tonic sent from Edward Cassidy, his nephew. Dr. Howell's Tonic. I was about to swallow it when I noticed a particularly foul smell."

"All medicines taste and smell foul," Prescott said, frowning as he examined the vial. "Did you swallow any of it?"

"No, instead I gave it to one of the geese near the house. The next morning I found it dead."

Prescott's frown deepened. "Did you tell Fenley?"

"I told him what I thought. I bade him take no more of any elixir his nephew might send him. He showed me other bottles that had come during the previous months."

"Had he taken any?"

"Fortunately, no. His frugality is legendary as you know, sir. He was determined to use up every drop of the tonic he had opened—one that the vicar had given him. I poured all the tonics out except for that vial which I give to you."

"I shall have it tested straight away," Prescott said. "You were right to come to me."

"I know your father's friendship with Fenley, sir. Do you think we should do anything about Mr. Cassidy?"

"I shall take care of Cassidy," Prescott said, looking grim.

AN HOUR LATER, Andrew Whiting drew away from his laboratory apparatus with as stern an expression as Prescott had ever seen on his face.

"I can't tell until I do some further tests, but I'd wager it's belladonna."

"Do you mean the cosmetic?"

"Aye. It's supposed to give females that wide-eyed, appealing look. The look of a mooncalf is more like it," he snorted. "And so they are, because it kills them after a time, but slowly unless they give up the eye-drops. But to have someone swallow it in such a dose!" He shuddered. "That would be murder.

"I'll proceed with the other tests, if you like."

"Yes, do. I'd appreciate it, Andrew," Prescott said.

Ten minutes later he pulled up at the Cassidy residence and overrode the protests of the butler and one of Edward's cronies that Mr. Cassidy was unwell.

When Prescott entered, Edward was reclining on a daybed, his face bruised and battered. Rehagen's thug had done his work well.

Edward grimaced. "What are you doing here, Prescott? Spreading sympathy to the ill?"

"Why shouldn't I?" Prescott retorted, drawing up a chair. "I understand from your Uncle Fenley that you've been doing so yourself. In fact, you have been so solicitous of his health that it behooves me to be equally solicitous of yours. I have here a bottle of that fine tonic you sent him some months ago from London."

Edward paled. "I don't need a tonic."

"Don't let the bad smell fool you," Prescott said bracingly. "This is capital stuff."

"Here now, what are you doing?" Two swollen eyes widened in alarm.

"Do you have a spoon, or perhaps a cup would be better. The more you take the quicker you heal."

"Just leave it."

"Oh, no. I mean to see you swallow this medicine before I leave the room. Oh, there's a cup on your table." He reached for it. "How shortsighted of me not to have seen it earlier." Lord Prescott poured some of the tonic into the cup and handed it to Edward. "Drink it up, lad."

"No!"

"My dear fellow, don't be so doltish. Don't you trust the tonic you sent your own uncle?"

"Not feeling quite in the pink."

"That's precisely why you need the tonic."

"No!"

"Don't be a gudgeon. It's just medicine."

"I don't want it."

"Your beating has unhinged you. I understand that the tonic is good at curing such an ailment."

"No, it is not!" Edward shouted. He threw off his blanket and stood in his nightshirt. "I order you out of my room. I don't want your poisonous tonics."

"Obviously demented. A taste of the tonic will right that in a trice."

"No. Keep that cup away from me!"

"Why?" Prescott asked, his voice hardening. "Is it because you know it is poison? That you yourself put the poison in it. Belladonna, is it not?"

"No—I didn't mean . . ."

"Then drink it up."

Edward wavered and picked up the cup. Then he put it down, his face red with shame. "I thought a little would make him sick enough . . ."

"Enough to die so you would inherit his money?" Prescott asked witheringly.

"He's an old man. He should die," Edward said edgily. "I've been waiting forever, do you hear? What a day this has been! First that chit Maria tells me that she has been lying to me all the while. She doesn't have a sou. Then Rehagen's man attacks me. And now..."

"And now I inform you that the game is up. Your uncle knows that you have been doctoring his tonic. I feel sure that he will change his will shortly and disinherit you."

Edward licked his lips. "But why would Uncle do such a thing?"

Prescott clucked his tongue. "He might not want to encourage you to poison him again. You are not thinking clearly, Edward. And I daresay that Mr. Rehagen might find his good will vanishing along with your future prospects. I might visit him and tell him so myself."

"You can't mean any of this," Edward quavered. "You wouldn't."

"Indeed I would. So I advise you to flee to the Continent, and never to set foot in England again."

"That's out of the question. I'll do no such thing!"

Prescott shrugged. "As you wish. I daresay that Mr. Rehagen might send a more capable fellow than the one who waylaid you this morning. Then again, maybe it will be just a bullet in the heart some evening when you are stepping out of your residence. Much cleaner, all in all, a bullet in the heart. Although there *is* the blood to mop up."

"All right. All right. I shall do as you say. I'll go and live on the continent. But how will I get there—I have no money."

"I shall have a ticket on the next packet to France delivered to you."

"What shall I do there? How will I live?"

"I have no idea," Prescott said in a bored tone. "I said I had a solution to this dilemma, not to any you might face when on the Continent."

"You think you've won, don't you, Prescott?" Edward said bitterly. "With me out of the way, you can marry Maria."

Prescott stared at the other man. "Maria? Don't be a fool. I don't want Maria. My secretary will deliver the ticket. You'd better start packing."

CHAPTER NINETEEN

"How could I have been such a fool as to have liked Edward Cassidy?" Eleanor said as she and Diana drove toward yet another sitting with Armand.

"He fooled everyone," Diana replied. "It's just fortunate that your father discovered the truth."

"Yes," Eleanor said, giving the reins a shake. She was not inclined to credit Sir Donald with much perception, but he had certainly scotched that match.

As their carriage clattered to a halt on Bond Street, Diana nudged her with an elbow. "Speaking of Mr. Cassidy, there he is."

Eleanor glanced sharply to the right where Edward was just coming out of Mr. Locke's shop. Far from shirking under their scrutiny, Edward lifted the beaver felt which Mr. Locke had just sold him. He was still fuming at Prescott's interference in his life. Catching sight of Eleanor, he recalled how Prescott had dealt him a facer for remarks about her. Maybe he could sow some mischief in the brief time remaining to him.

Boldly, he sauntered over to the carriage which had stopped in the crush of traffic.

"Good day, Miss Whiting, Mrs. Hawthorne."

Neither women replied to his greeting.

He managed to look momentarily abashed. "You are right to turn me the cold shoulder. My courting of Maria was not an honourable deed."

His confession startled the ladies.

"I'm glad you realize that," Eleanor said.

"Of course I was not the only one doing the deceiving."

Eleanor shifted uncomfortably in the carriage, well aware of the deception Lady Vyne had instigated concerning Maria's fortune.

"If you mean Maria's fortune . . ." she began.

"I don't mean Maria's duplicity, but Prescott's."

"Prescott's!"

Edward pinched a speck of dust from the beaver felt in his hands. "Yes, he was the one who bade me fix an interest in Maria. He knew my financial situation was worsening daily, and he said Maria would be the perfect answer."

Diana spoke up. "Nonsense. Lord Prescott was fixing his interest in Maria himself."

"That was mere flourishing. He and I agreed to act as rivals for her hand, and he agreed to let me win her. Now that he knows she has no fortune, I daresay he will drop her, too."

Eleanor had already detected a certain cooling between Prescott and her cousin.

"Lord Prescott doesn't need a fortune, bogus or real," Diana protested.

"No man turns up his nose at the prospect of a rich wife," Edward said.

"Move there, you in front!" an angry coachman called from behind.

Edward moved away from the carriage. "Good day to you, ladies," he said and went off, smiling maliciously to himself.

The story Edward had planted remained in Eleanor's mind long after Diana had finished her sitting with Armand and they were enjoying some of Mr. Gunter's ices.

"Diana, do you think it's true what Edward told us today—that Prescott knew he was in dire financial straits, that he was a fortune hunter and that he set him on Maria?" Eleanor said in a tone as sober as her look.

"Well it is most unlike Prescott," Diana pointed out, "but if it troubles you, why don't you simply ask him."

"I just might," Eleanor said grimly.

MARIA WHITING UTTERED A SIGH as she stared out the window of her bedchamber. She wondered if she were going to miss Edward. But as she thought the matter through, she found she did not really care. In fact she was relieved that she would not have to marry Edward. He had frightened her, and she would rather not marry a man who frightened her.

"Maria? Where are you?" Lady Vyne's voice floated up the stairs.

"Here, I am, Aunt."

"You have a caller. Hurry down!"

Maria peered quickly into a pier glass. Maybe it was Harry Addison. He had promised to call today to see how she was. Quickly she went down the stairs, coming to a halt when she saw her father.

"Papa!"

"Maria!" Mr. George Whiting tightened his arms about his daughter's shoulders.

"Oh, Papa, it is good to see you."

Mr. Whiting, a lanky man with an unruly shock of grey hair, was pleased to see his daughter looking none the worse for her broken heart. He was determined to take her home.

"I did my best for her," Lavinia had protested when he had arrived minutes earlier.

"I know," George said. "But I think that I shall have to take her back to the country."

"Take her back? But she is a notable hit here. She has many admirers. George, don't do anything hasty."

"It's not hasty. I've missed her. I think she'll be better at home with me."

Now, however, Mr. Whiting sat alone with his daughter, absorbing her tears on his best coat of Bath-blue superfine and acknowledging that to be in love was a very arduous undertaking, particularly when it came to naught.

"Which is why I'm here, my dear. I've come to take you back home."

Maria's tears dried miraculously. "Take me back, Papa? But why?"

Mr. Whiting lifted a brow. "Haven't you been crying to me about your broken heart?"

"I'm not really brokenhearted, just a trifle down-cast. Not really in the dismals, as Eleanor would say. Did Aunt Lavinia ask you to take me home?"

"No, it was my idea."

"When will you take me back?"

"Well, I have some business in London. Lavinia has agreed to put me up. So perhaps a week?"

"Just a week?" Maria gasped.

"You have had nearly six weeks in London," her father reminded her. "Come now, don't look so Friday-faced. I've brought a letter from your mother," he said, which led to the inevitable questions about the brothers and sisters she had left behind in the country.

At Mrs. Edgewater's ball on Saturday evening Mr. Whiting had an opportunity to view firsthand his daughter's obvious popularity in London circles. He had long been acquainted with the Edgewaters and was invited to accompany Maria to the ball. He was gratified to see that Maria's bungled romance had not caused anyone to shun her, and in fact the sprigs were tripping over themselves to pay her court.

"How can you think of taking her away?" Lady Vyne scolded. "See how they dangle after her."

"They are a bunch of puppies," Mr. Whiting observed through his quizzing glasses. "Where is that paragon you have spoken of to me, Prescott. Is that he?" he asked, nodding toward the only gentleman he could call something other than a pup, who was leading Maria out in a waltz.

Lavinia choked. "Heavens no, that is not Lord Prescott. That's Harry Addison. The idea of your confusing him with Prescott."

"Is Addison a beau of hers? How is it you've not mentioned his name?"

"Because he's not. He's a beau of Eleanor's—or he would be, if she would say yes to his offer. No, if it's Prescott you wish to see, that is he by the doorway."

Mr. Whiting turned his head and saw the tall, elegant gentleman kissing Mrs. Edgewater's powdered cheek. So this was Maria's conquest, was it? He made it a point to keep an eye on this Lord Prescott.

His lordship had intended only a token appearance at his aunt's ball, but Mrs. Edgewater was not about to let him escape so quickly.

"You are to take me in to supper," she ordered.

"I am always at your disposal, Aunt Judith."

"No, you're not." She rapped him on the knuckles with her fan. "Go and talk with one of those pretty girls over there."

"That would be an unendurable penance," Prescott said, fighting shy of any such action. From the addled looks thrown his way by several females just out of the schoolroom he knew that even to say a word to one of them would raise impossible expectations.

Maria passed, partnered in a waltz by Harry Addison, and she bestowed a shy smile on Prescott. He felt a surge of satisfaction. At least Edward Cassidy would no longer cause her mischief.

Unconsciously his gaze swept over the faces in the ballroom, as though searching for something. Then he saw Eleanor and he knew what he was waiting to see. She looked divine, in a breathtaking azure-blue silk, standing as straight and tall as possible talking to Julia and Andrew Whiting. The unmistakable urge to run his fingers through that mane of copper-coloured curls nearly overcame him. He was a stupid fool. She had made plain her disgust of him that night at Vauxhall Gardens and was now practically betrothed to Addison.

What further proof did he need—an invitation to their wedding? A grim smile spread over Prescott's face. No, he'd refuse that invitation all right, but he would dance once more with Eleanor, if only to hold her one last time in his arms.

He strolled over toward the Whitings, and saw Andrew's quizzical expression.

"Hallo, Prescott," he greeted. "Your aunt tells me she has decided to give Oakmore to the Church."

"Such is her scheme," Prescott replied. "Mrs. Whiting, Miss Whiting."

"Good evening, my lord," Julia said, wondering what was afoot and whether Prescott was still nursing his tendre for Eleanor.

"Miss Whiting, I wonder if I might ask for the next waltz."

"I'm afraid that I am promised to Major Bentley."

"Fiddle, Eleanor," Julia interjected. "Major Bentley isn't even here this evening."

"Perhaps you are afraid of dancing with me," Prescott said.

Eleanor put up her chin, goaded by his words. "I am afraid of no one, my lord."

"Good," he said, taking her hand and leading her out in the waltz.

She had forgotten what an excellent dancer he was, and for a few minutes gave herself up to the sheer delight of dancing with him. From across the room she could see Mrs. Edgewater and Lady Constance beaming at them. Hastily she stiffened her back.

"What's amiss?" he asked at once.

"Nothing..." Her eyes locked with his. Why was he so handsome? She would not succumb to his charms. Resolutely, she brought back to mind all his flaws. His treatment of poor Aimée. The way he had encouraged Edward to dangle after Maria.

"Maria seems to have recovered from her unhappy romance," Prescott observed now.

"Yes, lucky for her. Some other females would not have recovered so well. They might have gone into a decline."

"Poor sort of female they would have been," Prescott observed.

"You haven't paid your respects to her," she observed. "Are you no longer dangling after her?"

Wondering if this was a sign of interest, he looked down closely.

"No," he said softly. "I have no further interest in Maria."

Eleanor's lips curled. No, now that the joke was over. Now that Edward had done his mischief he would no longer find amusement in pursuing Maria.

"It was a cruel joke, Prescott," Eleanor said.

He stared down at her, aghast that she had seen so clearly that he was dangling after Maria to make her jealous. Seeing obvious pain in her eyes, he was stricken with remorse.

"My dear, I swear to you, I didn't think it would hurt anyone. Maybe just twit you a bit."

The gall of the man. He'd systematically set out to break Maria's heart as a joke? He had no scruples.

"Edward Cassidy has left London, I believe."

"Bound for the Continent," Prescott agreed, seizing on this topic with some relief.

"You've seen him?"

"We had a few words."

Of course they would. They were such good cronies and would no doubt exchange considerable words on the hoax that had failed.

"You know all about Edward's financial affairs?"

"Why, yes," Prescott replied. Who was it that she thought had alerted Sir Donald.

"You knew he was a fortune hunter?"

"Yes, of course."

Her jaw tightened. So Edward hadn't been lying. Prescott had put him up to the joke. Despicable, despicable man.

The waltz ended.

"Eleanor, may I call tomorrow?"

"No. I never want to see you again. You have caused my family enough heartache and mischief to last a lifetime."

He held her wrist. "You don't mean it."

She snatched her hand back. "I do mean it, my lord." She said, and her eyes told him that she was telling him the truth.

Lord Prescott took refuge in the card room, scarcely noticing the passage of time, or the opponents who sat next to him.

Eleanor had spurned him again. He was angry at her and at himself for continuing to yearn for her. Blast her. He had done her family a service and she held it against him! He gave in to his devil, playing recklessly and not for chicken stakes, either.

"There is no beating you tonight, Prescott," Philip Hawthorne murmured as he threw down his losses on the table. "I shall leave you and Mrs. Whiting to your cards."

Prescott glanced up. The card room had cleared and other than Philip, a cheerful observer, only Julia Whiting and himself remained. His luck had come and gone, while hers, he noticed now by the pile of money on the table, had been mostly good. Did she have enough to redeem all her debts before her husband discovered what she was up to? Thinking of Andrew brought Eleanor to mind, and his mood darkened.

"You are in a gambling mood, Mrs. Whiting?"

"If you are, my lord," Julia said, her success at cards making her less cautious than usual. Prescott's reputation at cards was nearly equal to his reputation at swords.

"What say you to this, one cut each of the deck, the highest card wins?"

"Agreed. But what will be the wager?"

"Everything on the table."

"Everything?" Julia looked up in alarm. She did not like the expression on Prescott's face.

"By Jupiter, Prescott," Philip protested.

Prescott ignored him. "You have ten thousand pounds there?"

"Yes."

"I have eight thousand here," he said, pushing a handful of bills at her. "I am two thousand short. Would this make up the difference?" he asked, putting down a spider-shaped ruby pin.

Julia gasped as she recognized the Whiting heirloom.

"Is the bet on?" he demanded.

She knew she ought to say no to this last wager. She could buy the pin from him. But what if he didn't wish to sell it? Eleanor had always said he was a contrary sort of man.

"Very well."

Prescott handed the cards to Philip. "Shuffle and deal them, will you, Philip?"

Muttering, Hawthorne did as he was asked.

"One card to Mrs. Whiting and one to myself," Prescott ordered.

Julia looked at her card. It was a knave of hearts. She felt giddy with excitement. She turned it over and waited. Prescott stared at the card in his hand. Then he gave a rueful smile and tossed it face down.

"You've won, Mrs. Whiting."

Julia jumped from her seat, unable to contain herself. She had won a high-stakes match with Prescott! But, more importantly, she had the Whiting pin back. Quickly, before she lost it, she put it in her reticule, which was stuffed near to bursting with the money she had won. The first thing she would do tomorrow would be to pay off everyone she owed. The second thing would be to send Aunt Lavinia the hideous pin.

"You will excuse me, I hope," Julia said, quickly leaving the card room.

Philip stared at Prescott, whose expression was unreadable. His friend did not look happy, which was understandable in a man who had lost more than ten thousand pounds. But he had forced the game on Mrs. Whiting.

"Cheer up, Prescott. You'll win it back."

"You can't win everything back," Prescott said. He rose to his feet and sauntered out of the room.

Hawthorne was about to follow. Then he saw the card that Prescott had tossed aside. Curious, he picked it up. His eyes widened. Queen of clubs.

CHAPTER TWENTY

"AUNT LAVINIA, is this the brooch you wished to examine?" Julia asked, handing the ruby pin over to Lady Vyne during a morning visit with Lady Constance.

"Thank you, my dear, but I merely wanted a look at it," Lady Vyne said. "And now that I have seen it I know it just won't do."

Julia felt increasingly vexed. To think of all the fuss and botheration she had been put to because of that stupid brooch. She gave vent to her frustration to Eleanor later when Lady Vyne had departed and Lady Constance had withdrawn to her sitting room with her sketching pad.

"It is annoying," Eleanor agreed. "Repairing the clasp and asking the craftsman to do it quickly to get it in Aunt Lavinia's hands, and then she only glances at it."

"It wasn't out to repair," Julia confessed. "I sold it to cover my losses."

"Good heavens! And do you now mean that you bought it back and are even more in debt?"

Julia laughed. "No, Eleanor. You see me totally free of debt. I have just paid off the moneylenders with interest. And never will I fall into their clutches again. I won ten thousand pounds and the ruby pin last night playing cards with Lord Prescott. He insisted on the game. I didn't wish to risk all my winnings, but I am glad I did because I paid off everyone. I must own, though, that at the time my hand was shaking."

"You say you won the pin from him. How did he get it?"

Julia shrugged. "Edward Cassidy sold it for me to a man named Grimes. I daresay Edward told him that."

Eleanor nodded. She had momentarily forgotten Prescott and his tie to Edward.

"But if he had won you would have been destitute."

"Yes, I know," Julia said naively, "but he didn't. I won. And I have learned my lesson. I shan't sit down to cards with anyone ever again, even for chicken stakes. I have learned my lesson."

"CAN YOU IMAGINE Prescott doing such a thing as to insist on Julia playing cards with him?" Eleanor asked Diana later that day. Mrs. Hawthorne had summoned her for the unveiling of her portrait.

"Philip told me all about it. Julia was lucky. The light in this corner doesn't make me look too hideously sallow, does it?" she asked anxiously.

"You look delightful."

"I hope so. Philip is in for a surprise when he sets foot in the door. Now come into the music room. I want to play my latest composition for you."

The two ladies settled at the pianoforte. "I still don't like Prescott bullocking Julia that way."

"If he hadn't, she wouldn't have won," Diana pointed out, searching for her music sheets.

"He probably wished to lure her even deeper in debt."

"Prescott lost to Julia deliberately. Philip turned over his card later. Prescott held a queen of clubs. Julia held only a knave of hearts."

Eleanor stared at Diana. "But why should he do such a thing?"

Diana gave a little smile. "Oh, Eleanor. The answer is as plain as two pins. Just think of all he has done for you and your family of late."

"Aside from this deliberate loss to Julia, what has Prescott done for us?" Eleanor demanded.

Mrs. Hawthorne threw her a despairing glance. "Why, you must know he alerted your father to the danger of Edward Cassidy."

"What!"

Diana looked surprised. "Oh, you didn't know." She looked suddenly guilty. "I forgot Philip swore me to secrecy about that."

"Well, I swear that I shall throttle you, Diana, if you do not tell me all."

Threatened with such a dire fate, Mrs. Hawthorne willingly complied. "Lord Prescott uncovered evidence that Edward was a fortune hunter and a wastrel, so he told your father. Didn't Sir Donald tell you?"

"No," Eleanor said, but she meant to find out.

SIR DONALD STARED GLOOMILY at his daughter, who had descended upon him looking in one of her freakish moods. And he was due to meet George at White's in ten minutes.

"I vow, no more about Edward. It's a closed chapter."

"I must know who told you about his being a fortune hunter."

"No one of importance," he said, edgily. No doubt she would throw a fit at Prescott's audacity in interfering.

"Was it Prescott?" she asked. "Papa, please. Tell me!"

He looked up, confused by the heartfelt emotion in her words. Eleanor appeared flushed and out of sorts. Sir Donald sighed. "Don't get on your high ropes. Prescott came by to tell me information on Edward's finances and bad dealings. I listened to him and made my own enquiries."

"So he did tell you."

"Aye. He said he didn't like to do it beforehand. Thought that Maria would never believe him, but couldn't let such an innocent marry Cassidy. There's been talk that Edward has a cruel streak when it comes to women. That's one of the things he unearthed."

Eleanor made no answer, merely standing with a strange expression on her face. Sir Donald wondered if she was even listening to him.

"He mentioned that he had told you several times that Edward might not be a match for Maria," he said quietly.

"So he did," she murmured.

Sir Donald wisely said no more and went off to his meeting while Eleanor drifted up to her bedchamber. Picking up a silver-handled brush, she began to pull it through her hair. Clearly Prescott had done her family considerable service. Edward had lied about his being in on the scheme to hand Maria to a fortune hunter. She now saw clearly that Edward had tried to besmirch Prescott's name. Prescott, who had saved Maria from a fatal marriage, who had given Julia the means to pay off her debts. But why? Was it possible that his declaration at Vauxhall Gardens was sincere? That he still loved and wished to marry her?

MADAME FANCHON reached for a pin just as a voice called out gaily in French from the front room. Eleanor and Diana were both being fitted with new gowns. But when Eleanor heard that voice, she froze.

Aimée Martine. She would know that voice anywhere.

"Excusez-moi, mademoiselle," Fanchon said and swept out of the back room. A swift exchange of French soon followed. Privately, Eleanor wished that she had paid more attention to her lessons in French.

The curtain was flung open once again as Fanchon returned.

"Was that Mademoiselle Martine?" Eleanor asked, turning from the looking glass in a deliberately off-hand way.

"Oui, she came by to pick out her trousseau. I told her to come back in an hour."

"Trousseau!" Diana gave a startled cry. "Is she to be married, then?"

Fanchon bobbed her head, her fingers busy with the lace trim on the shoulder of the dress.

"So she claims," Fanchon shrugged. "I might suspect her of lying since females in her profession often fool themselves that someone will marry them in the end, but in all the years that I have been gowning her she has never even mentioned marriage before. Aimée never lacked for sense."

"Is she happy about the pending nuptials?" Diana asked.

Fanchon nodded. "So happy she did not even scold when I told her to come back in an hour. And if I want to finish by then you must stand still, Madame Hawthorne," she informed Diana who obediently stood as still as a stock.

Eleanor too stood obediently for the modiste when her turn came, but her mind was far from quiet.

Aimée to marry? But whom would she marry, unless...Prescott?

"Prescott!" Diana whooped with laughter later when Eleanor divulged this suspicion during the carriage ride home. "No gentleman marries his mistress. It would cause such an uproar in the ton."

"Prescott has never flinched at causing a scandal," Eleanor retorted. "Besides, he might have good reason for marrying Aimée if she were breeding."

"Well, perhaps," Diana conceded. "But it sounds most out of the ordinary."

"He has always been devoted to her," Eleanor reminded her friend, horrified as tears smarted in her hazel eyes. Indeed, his devotion to Aimée three years ago was what had ended their betrothal. And now he was marrying her.

She dashed her tears away quickly with the back of her hand, hoping that Diana had not seen her. It was too stupid to be crying over Prescott when he was no longer part of her life.

Neither, as it turned out, was Harry Addison. This she discovered later at Hookam's where he and Maria were searching the shelves together. The guilty expression on their faces when Eleanor called their names clearly showed that they had more on their minds than the latest Walter Scott.

Harry was the reason that Maria was no longer languishing after Edward. They were in love with each other.

"Please, don't hate me, Cousin Eleanor," Maria beseeched.

"It's my fault entirely, Eleanor," Harry said chivalrously. "Maria did nothing to lure me on."

"Harry, how can you say such a thing! I did everything in my power," Maria declared hotly.

Eleanor laughed at them both. "How could she help it, Harry? You are so handsome, and she is so sweet. Indeed, anyone with half a brain would have seen what an excellent match you would make together long ago. I congratulate you. And—" she turned to her cousin and kissed her on the cheek "—I wish you both happy."

"I say, Eleanor, you are a veritable trump," Harry said, his arm tightening around Maria. "If you only knew how I was beginning to hate myself. Practically betrothed to you and yet falling top over tail in love with Maria."

"I suppose that is just my fate," she said with a laugh. "I am fated to be an ape leader."

Harry would be happier by far with Maria than with her, and Eleanor knew that he would dote on Maria. And to clinch the matter he was no fortune hunter, having a goodly income of well over ten thousand pounds a year.

"Which Uncle George should be pleased about," she told her mother that night when she went in to say good-night.

"Well, George is not such a purse-squeeze as to deny Maria Harry merely on the size of his income, but it is always pleasant to have a son-in-law who is well-pursed," Lady Constance said agreeably. "And there is no denying that one could not ask for a better-natured husband than Harry."

"If you continue talking in that manner, Mama, I shall begin to feel regret at losing him to Maria," Eleanor said with a rueful smile.

"Do you regret it?" her mother asked, clasping her hand.

"No. He is happy. Maria is happy. Everyone is as happy as a lark."

Lady Constance held her daughter's chin and gave Eleanor a searching look. "Including you, my dear?"

"Yes. I was just jesting about Harry. I don't want him."

"I know," her mother said gently. "But is there perchance someone you do want?"

Eleanor made a gallant effort at a smile. "It doesn't matter if I do, Mama," she whispered, feeling the tears fall as she sought the comfort of her mother's embrace.

CHAPTER TWENTY-ONE

AIMÉE TWIRLED HAPPILY around the room, the better to show off her new travel dress to Armand's admiring eyes.

"Ravishing, my dear," he said, sweeping her into his arms. "You will be the hit of Paris."

"And so will you," she said loyally. "Have you packed all your canvases?"

"Just the important ones. The others will be sold here. Sebastian has agreed to help me sell them. I will be taking them over to him now. Then when I return it's off to Dover for us!"

She kissed him goodbye, glad that he had an errand to run, for she had asked Prescott to call in an hour. She had a little present for him, a fob that she had bought in Rundell's. Over the years Prescott had given her so many trinkets and baubles that she was almost ashamed that this was the only thing she had ever given him. She hoped he would like it.

"Like it, Aimée? It is beautiful," he said, slipping his glass on the ribbon.

"I am glad," she said, looking pleased.

"But you shouldn't have. You and Armand will need the money in France."

"No, we won't, thanks to you. I know you are the one responsible for Armand's success. Generous-hearted Prescott . . ." She was overcome with emotion and kissed his hand.

He touched her fingers to his lips gently. "I wish you happy with him."

She smiled. "How goes your courtship of Eleanor Whiting?"

"She won't marry me. I've asked her twice."

"Then ask her again and keep asking until she says yes," Aimée urged.

Prescott shook his head, and a stubborn look came into his eyes. Aimée recognized it as being the same look of three years ago when he had told her about Eleanor returning his ring wrapped in muslin. No doubt he would wait another three years before speaking to her again.

There had to be something she could do for him and this Eleanor Whiting—but what?

HADLEY, THE BUTLER, coughed as he entered the sitting room where Eleanor sat, reading the latest of Miss Austen's splendid novels.

"What is it, Hadley?" she asked, looking up.

"You have a caller, Miss. Miss Aimée Martine."

Aimée Martine. Eleanor thrust aside her novel, her thoughts revolving like a Catherine wheel. What on earth could that woman want with her?

"Send her in," Eleanor said. She did her best to calm her nerves, as Aimée was ushered in, looking quite beautiful. Eleanor's eyes slid down to the tiny waist. Good heavens, she wasn't even showing yet. But then, some females didn't.

"Miss Whiting? I think it time you and I came to an understanding."

Eleanor marvelled at the other woman's audacity.

"An understanding about what?" she asked.

"About the man we both care so much for, Lord Prescott."

Eleanor tossed her head back. "Prescott is of no interest to me."

"Listen to me. He loves you. He told me so himself. How can you turn him away now?"

"Miss Martine, are you really urging me to take up with Prescott?" Eleanor asked, astonished.

"Yes."

"Your marriage makes no difference to either of you?"

"My marriage?" Aimée paused. "No, of course it does not. Prescott has his life. I have mine. But I want him to be happy, which he will be with you to love."

Eleanor fumed. "I have never heard so outrageous a suggestion in my life. You plan to marry Prescott and yet you advise me to become his *chère amie*."

"What?" Aimée stared for a moment, then she gave a whoop of laughter. "*Mon Dieu*, I am not marrying his lordship! I am marrying Armand Saint Jacques, the painter."

"Armand. Oh!" Eleanor stared at her, relieved and yet disappointed. Of course Prescott would arrange things so that Armand would marry Aimée and she could bear the babe quietly.

"Is it Prescott's doing?" she asked, walking toward the bay window.

"*Oui*. But Armand does not know."

"No, it would be difficult for him. But what will you say if the babe resembles Prescott?"

Aimée gasped. "Babe?"

Eleanor turned on her heel and faced her. "Let us not peel eggs, Miss Martine. You came here to my residence, putting the most brazen proposal forward. Do you really think that I could love a man who would send his pregnant mistress away to be married off to another. No matter how good a face you put on it, that is what he is doing.''

"Pregnant mistress... Me?'' Comprehension flashed in Aimée's brilliant eyes. "You think I am *enceinte*? *Incroyable*. How came you by so foolish an idea?''

"You went down to the convent in Wiltshire.''

"*Oui.* I went on a mission. To find the girl that Edward Cassidy had seduced and left with child. I found her and brought her back to her lover, Sebastian. They have married and are happy.''

"You were using the Prescott travel chaise. Andrew, my brother, saw you himself.''

Aimée gave an understanding nod. "Ah yes, the one who blundered into the carriage. I assure you, Miss Whiting, that I am not with child. And I think that you are foolish if you continue to turn your back on Lord Prescott. He loves you.''

"Love did not keep him from continuing to see you three years ago.''

Aimée glanced meditatively down at the Wilton carpet. "It was my doing. He broke off our relationship. Furious, I vowed to find a way to bring him back to me and end his love for you. I knew you to be a young lady of high ideals. I knew you would not forgive him easily if you thought he'd deceived you. So I sent word to Prescott that I needed to speak to him on an important matter. I learned that you would be at Hampton Court and I arranged for our meeting to be seen. You threw him over, just as I knew you would. I won him back.''

"A most successful scheme," Eleanor said, tight-lipped.

"Oh yes, I had won him back, but—" she blinked back tears "—he was not the same man. I had won, but he still loved you. Even during those three years when no one dared mention your name to him, I knew he thought of you." She smiled sadly and wiped her eyes. "We have been friends these three years, Prescott and I, nothing more. They were difficult years for me, particularly when he would call out your name in his sleep as he lay next to me in my bed."

Eleanor gasped and felt a tug at her heart. "Is that true?"

"I would not lie about such a thing," Aimée replied. "I have my pride, too." She pulled on her gloves. "Now, I am bound to France with Armand, who waits for me. I tell you this because I feel you are foolish if you allow *your* pride to stand in the way of happiness. Lord Prescott was never the rake people claimed. But he is a proud man. He tells me that he has offered for you twice and will not a third time, so the next move is yours, Miss Whiting."

Aimée rose. Without hesitation, Eleanor offered her her hand. The Frenchwoman smiled and clasped it. Then, confident that she had done all she could in this matter, Aimée went off to meet Armand. Eleanor sank back on the velvet couch, her mind and heart in equal turmoil. Then, resolutely, she rose.

LORD PRESCOTT, returning to his residence after a night at the green baize tables of Watier's, found his butler, Neels, waiting up for him.

"Neels?" he enquired. "What the devil are you doing up? You should have been to bed long ago."

"I would have, my lord, except that I thought it incumbent upon me to wait until you arrived, particularly since you have a caller."

Prescott stared. "At this hour? It's past two."

"Yes, my lord, I know. She arrived at eight, and when I explained that you were out—" He got no further, for Prescott had pivoted at his words.

"She? It's a female, then?"

"Oh yes. I explained that you were not in, but she insisted upon waiting."

"You should have showed her the door," Prescott said, by no means pleased by the tale his servant was relating.

"I tried, my lord," Neels replied, accepting this stricture without a qualm.

"Evidently not hard enough," his employer said.

"My lord—" the butler felt roused to defend himself "—she began to disrobe. Well, really, my lord. I couldn't think what to do so I left her in the drawing room, and I came out here to wait for you."

"Really, Neels, a hurly-burly female descends and begins to take off her clothes—"

"Oh no, my lord, she's not a hurly-burly female. It's Miss Whiting."

The veins of his lordship's neck stood out wildly. "Miss Whiting?" he ejaculated and made at once for the blue drawing room. Eleanor—at this hour? Disrobed?

He paused at the threshold of the room and saw that, true to his butler's narrative, Eleanor sat, or rather lay there—for she had fallen asleep—garbed in a dress unbuttoned to the waist, exposing her white chemise.

Now what on earth was he to do? Prescott kicked a log on the fire. At the sound, Eleanor awoke.

"What is the meaning of this?" Prescott said, keeping his distance. She looked about her sleepily, not appearing to care that her hair was down along her shoulders.

"I'm glad you're here, Prescott, I wanted to see you."

"Which is more than I can say for you," he scolded. "Button your clothes. You should be at home. Do your parents know where you are?"

"I told them I was spending the night at Diana's." She made no move to button her dress.

"Eleanor, have you lost your wits?"

A smile lit up her eyes. "No, I seem to have regained them."

"You show up at my residence garbed in . . ."

"It is called a chemise," she said, a smile now evident on her lips. "It is the latest sleeping apparel for ladies."

"It is outrageous," Prescott said, struggling not to stare at the chemise through which he could discern her figure. "And so are you for being here with me dressed that way. You've lost your mind."

"It was the only way I could think of to get you to marry me. It stands to reason that a gentleman like yourself, entertaining a young lady of good reputation in such a state of undress would undoubtedly feel compromised. Unless you don't wish to marry me."

He grasped her by the arm and shook it. "Don't try to gammon me, Eleanor. I have had enough of hoaxes. Are you saying that you will marry me?"

"It seems the only course left me," she pointed out, the smile growing even broader, "since I am a lady and am definitely compromised in your own home."

"Fustian rubbish."

"Really, my lord, you are being needlessly obtuse. The matter would be obvious to a five-year-old. I am flinging myself at your head."

"Are you?" For the first time a smile touched Prescott's eyes as well as his lips. "And rake that I am, I'm expected to sit here and do nothing?"

"You are not a rake," she said slowly, one finger tracing the outline of his jaw. "Peter, I thought such improbable things about you. I have learned the truth from various sources." She dropped her hand. "But if I have misjudged things, if you no longer want me, if you no longer love me..." She looked up, uncertainly.

That uncertainty vanished in the next instant as, with a growl, Lord Prescott gathered her into his arms and kissed her. Wildly, he planted kisses on her face and neck; the pulse in her throat throbbed.

"This is the most foolish thing you have ever done," he said in a voice that sent a shiver of excitement through her.

"As foolish as sending you your ring back three years ago?" she asked.

"Yes. For if you stay here, looking like that for a moment longer, I shan't be responsible for my actions."

"Spoken like a true gentleman. Would I shock you if I told you that I was prepared for that eventuality?"

He drew away. "Eleanor?"

"Come along, my lord," she said matter-of-factly, now beginning to button her dress.

"What are you doing?" he protested. "Where are you going?" he demanded, following her out of the room.

"I asked Neels to send a carriage to the front as soon as you came in. He is so excellent a manservant that I trust we will now find the carriage waiting." She opened the door. "I was right.

"I have had enough of betrothals to you. We marry by special licence at the border."

"And your parents?" he quizzed, knowing full well that he should dispatch the carriage back to Mount Street with her in it.

"I left them a note and asked them to send our announcement in to the *Gazette*."

"So I am about to step into parson's mousetrap, am I?" Prescott asked, looking at her in that daunting fashion.

"If you would be good enough to assist me in," she said, "and follow me."

"With the greatest of pleasure, Miss Whiting," Prescott replied, handing her in and stepping boldly into the carriage. She had no time to get settled in the vehicle because he pulled her once again into his arms and kissed her so thoroughly that she was rendered breathless and unable to order Walter to set off.

"Prescott," she murmured, when she could speak. "The horses."

"What about them?" he asked, much more interested in the way her ear resembled a seashell than in his Welshbreds.

"They're not moving," she said, her eyes warm with laughter. "We are still standing in front of your residence."

"So we are," he said, giving in to the temptation and kissing her ear. Then he leaned his head out the window of the vehicle.

"Walter?" he called out. "Are you still there?"

"Yes, my lord!"

"To Gretna Green. And don't interrupt us until we have arrived there."

"Very good, my lord," Walter replied, with a broad grin, as the horses at last set off.

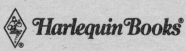

Harlequin Regency Romance™

Romance the way it was *always* meant to be!

The time is 1811, when a Regent Prince rules the empire. The place is London, the glittering capital where rakish dukes and dazzling debutantes scheme and flirt in a dangerously exciting game. Where marriage is the passport to wealth and power, yet every girl hopes secretly for love....

Welcome to Harlequin Regency Romance where reading is an adventure and romance is *not* just a thing of the past!